# Gladys

# Gladys

Trudy Weiss

2021

*To Grandma,*
*your quilts, recipes, and legacy*
*still tell your story.*

# Contents

# Chapter One | Realization

*1922*

Gladys mopped the sweat from her eyes with a dishrag. She felt so hot, grease - splattered, and she smelled like fried chicken. Everybody had forgotten about her.

"Everybody likes to eat, but nobody wants to clean up," she muttered. Maybe just this once Daisy or Ivy would come and wipe the dishes or put something away. But they were too busy curling their hair and fixing themselves up for the picture man to remember to help.

You would think Ma would check on her. But she heard Ma's soft voice chiding Jack and Clarence to not mess their clothes. "Play with him, Clarence," Ma said, "and keep him happy."

Gladys poured hot water into the rinse pan from the kettle on the stove. She dunked the knives and forks. The pots still needed cleaning and the picture man was due in a quarter of an hour.

Pa would strap her if she didn't have the dishes done. He never forgot about her, though at times she wished he would. He always found her whenever anything was out of place or missing.

The front of her apron was soaked, and her hair was matted around her neck. She felt ugly. If she couldn't be born pretty, why couldn't she learn to be pretty?

She had begged Daisy and Ivy to straighten her hair with the curling iron or trim her frizzy bangs, but they said there wasn't a whole lot they could do.

Sometimes when Ma looked at her, she would just sigh. Gladys wondered what was behind the sighing.

She picked up a pot and took more of the slimy, soft soap and salt to scrub it when Bud came into the kitchen.

Untying her apron, he said, "Go get ready Bit; I'll finish up in here."

"Thanks Bud," she rinsed her hands in the sink and scooted out the swinging door.

Finally, she could get ready.

As she dashed up the stairs, Gladys heard a knock and saw the picture man and his assistant through the glass of the front door. Pa answered and they bustled in with their equipment and began to set up in the dim living room. The dark green window shades were drawn closed, and the prickly horsehair sofa sat between the two windows. The heavy floral curtains made a pretty frame on either side. Her family was already dressed and gathered.

Gladys ran into the room she shared with Daisy and Ivy. Her Sunday best dress lay on the floor. Stockings, silk sashes and ribbons were scattered over the four-poster bed.

She looked at the wash basin and pitcher on the stand near the window and wished she had time for a sponge bath. She felt so alone. The mirror mocked her as she stripped to her shift and struggled into her dress. No one was there to fasten the buttons or tie her ribbons.

Gladys reluctantly came down the stairs, knowing her efforts would be inadequate. Her brown hair framed her face like a halo, and she could not button up the back of her dress by herself.

Pa and Ma sat on the sofa with Baby Jack. Pa noticed her first.

"Mattie, do somethin' with that girl to make her presentable." Turning away he cleaned his nails with a jackknife.

Ma looked at her and exclaimed, "Gladys, come here and lemme straighten you out."

"Yes, Ma," she shuffled over and looked at Daisy and Ivy. They were so pretty and fashionable with their curls arranged on top of their heads.

Ma rummaged through her work basket, found a brush, and tried running it through her mass of tangles.

"Never mind, we'll just pull your hair back and tie a big bow atop your head," Ma sighed and gave her a hug.

14

"Wash your face and don't be all day about it." Pa's harsh voice interrupted them and startled her. She was enjoying Ma's cool hands on her neck and the closeness of her touch.

She scurried to the kitchen and wiped her face on a damp dish towel.

The picture man and his assistant were about finished setting up the tripod with the big camera and bellows. He ducked his head under the black cloth in back and adjusted the front lens while his assistant measured flash powder onto a handheld plate.

When Gladys came back, Pa's unsmiling eyes swept over her and he clucked his tongue. She turned and walked to stand with Bud.

"How're you doin', Bit?" Bud asked and gave her a little hug.

Pa called him shiftless because he wanted to join the rodeo and didn't want to stay on the farm. She leaned against him and sniffed. He always smelled of horses, leather and far off places. She felt lonely and knew he'd be leaving home soon.

"Take me with you, Bud," she whispered.

Gladys knew at eleven she was too young to leave, but Bud always made her feel good, like maybe she was as good as everybody else.

"We're all set." The photographer said and began arranging the family around Pa and Ma. Jack sat in Ma's lap; Clarence leaned against Ma in between his parents. Bud stood in the back with Ivy and Daisy on either side. Gladys leaned away trying to blend with the curtains. She looked at the camera and prayed that somehow that box would make her beautiful.

She stared at the lens. In her mind's eye, the family's reflection stared back at her. Her brothers and sisters looked more like her mother with eyes the color of a mossy creek or dark blue sky and brown hair. Her own reflection was of an awkward, gangly girl with eyes so pale blue they almost seemed without color. Her hair frizzed around her head. Gladys knew why she was judged so harshly by her own father; she wasn't pretty.

# Chapter Two | Mattie

*1911*

Mattie often wondered about James. He worked hard in the fields and every year they had an extra calf or two to sell, but there was no denying his moods and downright meanness at times. She knew when the darkness overcame him it was best to keep the children and the chickens away from his angry feet. She sighed and picked up Gladys and put her to her breast.

She loved to watch James and Bud strutting around the farm; Bud tried so hard to keep up with his Pa's long-legged stride. James was burnt red from the sun. The sun beat down on his fair complexion. His big hat, long sleeved shirt and kerchief provided him with little protection from being in the sun so much.

Mattie kept thinking. Her other three children were bald as chicken eggs until they turned one and then soft duck down like curls covered their heads. This child at four months had a mop of wild, curly hair and colorless light blue eyes that stared back at her as she rocked, nursed and puzzled out secrets.

She thought back to the fall of 1896, fifteen years earlier when James rode into town on his big horse. He was lean and dusty from working cattle ranches in eastern Oklahoma. All the girls stopped talking as he rode by the school yard at noon. After school, she hurried home to work in her family's store before supper and there he was. She hurried over to wait on him.

His eyes traveled over her figure before he placed his order of snuff and two shirts to be made to order. Pa told him the shirts would be ready on Friday, two days from now.

"Where can I rent a room and get somethin' to eat?" He asked Pa while looking at her.

"Mae lets rooms, and that includes board; she's three doors down. Mattie, help your Ma with dinner," Pa said with a look that silently told her to hold her tongue.

"It's too early Pa."

"Mattie, don't be sassin'."

"Okay Pa, anything else Mister ?" Her question hung in the air like a bad odor. She couldn't wait to tell the girls at school that she talked to this stranger.

"Call me, James, if it's okay with your Pa and I'll take a scoop of that hard candy." He pointed and light blue eyes crinkled. Pa grunted and turned his back to pick the calico cotton from the tall shelves running along the sides of the store. Mattie scooped some ribbon candy from the bin behind the glass counter, weighed it, and handed it to James.

"Here's your candy, Pa will put it on your tab. Would you like to pick out some fabric?" Mattie said.

"Why don't you pick out somethin' nice. Care for a piece?" James winked and held the sack open to her.

"Mattie, I ain't tellin' you again."

"I better run and help Ma, but I'm sure she'll make some shirts you'll like." Mattie quickly took a piece of candy and flashed James a smile. She opened the door in the back of the store that attached to the house. She kissed Ma on the cheek and found the cornmeal and other ingredients and started mixing cornbread.

"Ma, the nicest stranger came into the store and he gave me a piece of candy and wanted me to pick out shirt fabric for him," Mattie said breathlessly. "I want to invite him over for supper on Sunday since we always have somebody over and he don't have anyone to cook for him except Ol' Mae. He rode into town on the prettiest brown dappled horse. I can't wait to tell the other girls at school that I talked with him."

Ma stopped her work at the stove.

"Mattie, I'm surprised at you. I didn't raise you to be disrespectful; it's Miss Mae and I can't believe your Pa let you take candy from a stranger, let alone have a conversation with him. Keep in mind, you're but fifteen."

As she was speaking, the door to the store opened and Pa stomped through. He scowled at Mattie and sat down heavily.

"Ellen, your daughter was flirtin' like nobody's business. I was usin' words as well as looks to keep her from talkin'." Turning to Mattie he continued, "I'm goin' to be watchin'; no more flirtin' and when he's in the store, come back here until he leaves," Pa huffed. "We don't know nothin' about him and I ain't gonna have you talked about in this town. Keep your distance."

Mattie hung her head and asked, "Does this mean he can't come for Sunday dinner? We always have new people over and it don't seem fair that we don't invite him."

"NO! He ain't comin' to dinner," Pa exploded, "and I don't want to hear any more about him."

Pa's warning did little to discourage her. Mattie was the center of attention the next day as she talked to her friends.

"I kept after Ma until she said I could cut the button holes and sew the buttons on his shirts," Mattie said with pride. "I make tinier stitches than she does."

"Oh, we know you can sew," one of her friends teased, "before you know it, you'll be sewin' buttons on all his shirts and cookin' his hash."

Mattie blushed and then the school bell rang signaling lunchtime was over.

Mattie badgered her Pa until he agreed that James could court her. Ma and Pa had reservations because he was older and never talked about himself or where he came from. But after a while, everyone knew he was a hard worker and James was in demand for odd jobs and hauling freight from the depot.

Mattie loved him from the start and she knew he loved her, too. In spite of her folks, she invited him over for dinner that first Sunday. Every Lord's Day after that he came to church and afterwards ate dinner with them. He escorted her to socials and to box suppers to raise money for an addition to the school-house. James bid five dollars (almost a week's wages) on her decorated box and the privilege to share it with her. No other box even got two dollars. Some Sunday afternoons he rented a courting buggy and they drove all over the prairie.

Mattie and James married the day after school let out on her sixteenth birthday. Not long after the wedding, a man named Doc came to the door and said he needed to see Joe Simmons.

Pa rubbed his chin, "I don't know no Joe Simmons, but my daughter married James Simmons. He hauls freight and don't talk much. Two streets over, the yellow house on Third Street."

"Thank you kindly," Doc said and started towards the door.

Pa hollered after him, "Are you bringin' hard news?"

Doc turned and said, "I don't aim to be rude, but my business is my business." He touched his fingers to his hat and left.

Doc easily found the house in the small town. He paused before knocking and looked through the leaded glass window. It was late afternoon and James was home for the day, reading the newspaper aloud to Mattie as she knitted.

James opened the door in response to his knock.

"Hullo, Joe." Doc said.

James stepped out on the porch and slammed the door behind him, "She don't know. What're you doing here?"

"I came because your Ma's dead."

Mattie crept silently and perched underneath the bedroom window that opened out to the front porch.

She overheard Doc say, "They're both dead and . . ."

James spat out the words, "Good, the bastard's dead."

Doc continued, "Keep your shirt on. Cleta died six months ago. She lived on the farm and saved every cent. I knew you were in Oklahoma by the postmarks on the letters I delivered to her. I've been searching to give you what is rightfully yours."

Doc looked at the emotionless young man and continued, "I buried her by your brother, and I made sure she had a nice stone in the church yard, 'Loving Mother of James and Joe'."

Mattie put her hand to her mouth. She snuck away and went to the kitchen. She boiled water and filled a floral teapot with tea and hot water and placed it on a serving tray with cups and saucers from the cupboard. She poured milk into a pitcher and set sugar and cookies on the tray and walked onto the porch and greeted the doctor.

"Hey, I'm Mattie. It's nice to meet you."

She placed the tray on a small table and touched James on the shoulder. "You never told me you had a brother."

Doc Butler stood up, "Pleased to meet you, Mattie. I'm Doc Butler, Ma'am, and . . ."

James interrupted, "Mattie, go to your Pa's and wait until I come. I need to settle some things with Doc."

"But . . ."

"No, buts. You should go."

She ran all the ways with a thousand questions in her head. She decided to say as little as possible about what she overheard. She burst through the back door and said, "Ma, James is busy. Can I eat supper with you?"

"Anytime, Mattie," Ma said. "Pa did mention that a man came lookin' for him, but with a different first name. Do you know what's goin' on?"

"All I know is his name and he's from somewhere else." Mattie said and spying a pie she asked innocently, "Can I have a piece of pie, Ma? I love your buttermilk pie. Mine never turns out."

Distracted Ma replied, "Help yourself. Let's go over the recipe together and see why yours don't come out right. You know where the plates are, and I'll make some tea."

During supper Ma and Pa questioned her, but she kept the conversation centered on cooking, the store, or Elsie Fay's newest baby.

James never told her any details about the visit from Doc Butler. She never asked him either. Never one to talk much, he carried his passion and anguish into bed. She knew a deep sorrow existed inside of him and she was afraid of what his secret might be. Mattie was happy to oblige him with her body. Part of her wanted to share the stormy darkness that resided in his soul, but in the end, fear kept her from exploring the innermost recesses. So, she accepted the dark moods and anger that overcame him at times.

When Doc Butler left, they had a small sum of money to buy a vacant quarter section outside of town. It was their 160 acres and though it was not fertile bottom land; they watched the weather and held onto their dreams. James loved the land and Mattie loved him and all their children.

# Chapter Three | Gladys in the Morning

*1917*

Gladys opened one eye to gaze at the purple martin hopping along her windowsill. His feathers glittered dark purple, almost black in the sun, as he sternly looked at Gladys with his dark eyes as if to say, "Get out of bed sleepyhead, come outside."

At night, Daisy and Ivy, her two older sisters, giggled and whispered in the big, brass, feather bed that they all shared. She tried not to mind being left out of their conversations by taking comfort in the sights taking place outside her window. The birds and morning sounds welcomed her. During the early dawn the farmyard came to life as the calf bleated for his breakfast and the rooster crowed letting his harem of hens know he was still king of the coop. In the house, Ma clanged and banged the stove lids as she stirred the fire.

Gladys dressed in one of two workday dresses, joined Ma in the kitchen, and listened as she planned the day.

"I want to can tomatoes and maybe okra today. We came up short on vegetables last winter and I aim to put up as many as I can."

"I can help you Ma. I'm big enough now," Gladys said as she sipped her cambric tea. She was only six and this was a special treat she shared with Ma.

"I don't want Jack underfoot and close to the boilin' water when I set the jars to seal the lids," Mama said. "You need to watch him."

It was not her nature to complain, so she didn't argue or voice her true feelings. But why couldn't Daisy or Ivy watch Jack for once?

All too soon Pa and the boys clumped down the stairs and Gladys ran outside before Pa could see her. Whenever he came into the kitchen and she was there he stared right at her and remarked, "day's a wastin'." Never mind that Ivy and Daisy were not even up out of bed yet.

Pa expressed little affection or approval towards any of his children. But with a child's instinct, Gladys knew something about her bothered him more than the others. She tried not to mind because Mama always told her how much she enjoyed their special time in the morning and kissed her good night after prayers.

"Hey Bit," Bud called to her as he, Pa, and Clarence made their way to the barn.

"Hey Bud, Hey Clarence, Hey Pa," she called back as she opened the chicken pen.

Pa nodded but did not speak. Clarence in his little treble voice yelled back, "Hey."

She stepped inside the coop and rhymed:

> Here chickie, chickie, chickie
> A layin' in your nest,
> Give me your eggs,
> and eat your breakyfast.

Coming in through the back-door Gladys announced, "Look Ma, I found ten eggs today. The hens don't mind when I check the nests, as long as I don't spook 'em." She came into the farmhouse kitchen and placed her basket on the kitchen counter by the red-handled pump.

"You do have a way with those chickens," Ma said as she cut biscuits and put them in the buttered pan. "No one else can get them to lay like you do."

"They like the extra pepper I put in the mash." Gladys opened the oven door. "It makes me sneeze, but I do my sneezin' in the barn, before I feed 'em."

"That must be the secret to your success," Ma smiled.

When Ma sold her eggs in town, she collected seven cents a dozen from Mr. Eric at the store and sometimes gave Gladys a penny. Gladys bought a sucker and swapped licks with

Clarence or socked it away under her long underwear in her drawer of the old dresser she shared with her sisters.

Ma took the basket off the table. She went to the cool cellar that was the cold storage room and brought up the basket of eggs Gladys had collected earlier in the week. Ma cracked twelve eggs in a bowl, added milk, salt, pepper, and whipped the ingredients together and poured them into a sizzling skillet. She then gave the bubbling gravy on the back of the stove a quick stir.

Gladys left the bright, sunlit kitchen to set the table in the dining room for her family. Upstairs she heard Daisy and Ivy sweeping and making beds. Pa, Bud, and Clarence thumped in from the barn after seeing to the cows, pigs, and horses. She heard Bud open the cellar door and take the fresh milk down to cool. Baby Jack cooed in his crib and then started hollering. Ma called Gladys to bring him to her.

She glanced in the kitchen before she ran up the stairs. Breakfast smelled and looked so good. Ma's strawberry and apricot preserves glistened in the morning light. The cream, fresh milk and butter were ready on the kitchen worktable. She liked cantaloupe and gravy together, the saltiness of the gravy brought out the sweetness of the fruit.

"Daisy, Ivy time for breakfast," Gladys called to her sisters from her parent's room and scooped Jack up after changing his diaper. She followed her sisters downstairs and handed Jack to Ma. After quickly washing her hands she took her place at the table between Ma and Clarence.

Pa said grace. The family ate quickly without talking. Pa did not like chatter during meals. Jack finished nursing and Ma put him in his bed box and then she ate.

After breakfast, Gladys cleared the table and washed the dishes with Ma. Ivy and Daisy went to weed the kitchen garden and pick vegetables that were ripe.

"If you see any green tomatoes, I'll fry them for dinner," Mama hollered out the window to her two oldest daughters.

Pa and the boys were already out in the fields tending the baby watermelons. Pa was watching the weather and hoped it would hold for another week before he harvested the broom corn.

"Ow Ma, that hurts," Gladys cried out as she basted her head with water and apple cider vinegar before combing out her snarls.

"Be still Gladys," Ma said. "If you keep squirmin' I'll never finish and it's gonna hurt worse."

Gladys eyes watered from the pulling and the reproof. She silently handed her ribbon to Ma and wished her hair was easier to comb like her sisters'. Her hair was so curly and colorless that it looked like sprung bed springs.

"There now, all done. Keep neat and mind Jack for me. Go out on the porch and water the geraniums."

"Yes Ma," Gladys said.

Gladys moved Jack and the bed box to the porch. She pumped water into the tin watering can. The baby laughed and reached out when he saw her. Gladys put the watering can down and picked up her brother and went to the swing.

She whispered to him as she rocked, "Why did Ma get cross? I can't help the way I look." She looked down at her skinny legs and back to her brother's chubby legs.

"We sure look different you and me, Jack. You're so pretty."

Gladys laughed as Jack started to grunt and his face turned bright red.

"Woo-wee, for such a pretty baby you sure make a fearsome smell. You ain't so pretty now."

She took her brother upstairs and took off his dirty cloth and dropped it into the waste pail. From the clean wet pile of rags, she lifted his legs, wiped his bottom, powdered him with cornstarch, and secured a clean one with safety pens. She brought him and the pail downstairs. She would clean the mess later by dumping the solids in the outhouse and pouring more bleach and water on the dirty cloths as she set them to soak.

"I'm gonna wash my hands," Gladys said as she handed the baby to Ma.

"You're one for bein' clean after changin' him or goin' to the outhouse. Finish waterin' the plants and I'll feed Jack now," Ma said and unbuttoned her shirtwaist.

At the kitchen sink, Gladys let the stream of water run over her hands. She took a bit of the soft soap Ma had made from lye, fat and ashes, and then rinsed and dried her hands on the kitchen towel. Her heart felt lighter. Ma's smile made the day bright. She picked up her watering can and sprinkled water on the bright red tops of the geraniums set in tin cans on the steps. She sat in the swing and listened to the creek of the windmill as it brought up water for the stock pond, well, and kitchen pump. Her eyes took in the rose bushes that Ma valiantly watered and talked to in a weak attempt to keep them alive. She was usually rewarded with blooms in the spring.

"Someday they'll really bloom Gladys," Ma always said. "Some growin' things like people just take a little longer to get started."

Gladys stared at the bushes until her eyes teared, and then picked up her watering can and walked to the stock pond, not wanting to bother Ma inside the house. She decided maybe the roses would appreciate a little extra attention today.

# CHAPTER FOUR | TYPHOID

*1923*

The musty, yeasty smell of old bread filled the farm-house, the smell of typhoid. In a corner of the living room dirty linen lay waiting to be washed. A greenish watery trickle escaped to stain the wood floor.

Without warning, Ma, Ivy, and Clarence soiled them-selves day and night; no time to bring a bedpan. Clean sheets and night gowns were fouled faster than Gladys could fetch them off the clothesline. Sometimes the sick folks had to lay in their own mess until the laundry dried.

Dishes towered high in the sink. Flies buzzed around the dirty laundry and the food crusted dishes while, day and night, more floated in the huge iron pot of water steaming on the stove. Utensils, water, and linens were boiled to kill the invisible bacteria laying waste to her family.

Gladys gagged as she lifted the tub of dirty linen and kept her mouth shut as the flies buzzed around her face. She lugged it to a pit Pa had dug in the yard. Using a stick of fire-wood, she scraped off the solids and dumped the foul-smelling liquid from the tub. She threw in the stick and shoveled lye and dirt onto the contents.

She glanced at the sun and estimated it was mid-morning. She waited for Pa to come with the lye soap and buckets of boiling water from the stove. Gladys grabbed the washboard and wash tub hanging on the side of the house. Pa arrived and alternated between pouring cold water and boiling water into the washtub before she scrubbed the soiled linens with lye soap. He left while she worked but would be back to help her dump the dirty water into the pit before a boiling water rinse. Then everything would hang on the line to dry and sanitize.

Finished with the typhoid laundry by noon, she hollered at Pa to bring out the dirty clothes that the three of them wore.

Stripped to her shift and Pa and Jack to their union suits, she washed their clothes in the wringer washer and spread them to dry on the porch railings and furniture.

Since no one had time to water, skeletal stalks were all that remained of their crop of broom corn. The red geraniums and yellow rose bush had withered and died. Looking around all she could see was brown, and everything smelled of fear and disease.

Fright lodged in the hearts of both the caretakers and the dying. They all knew a mighty separation was coming, a pain too great to bear.

Her hands were sore, and she struggled to open jars of canned okra and corn. Too tired to cook they ate what was available from the cellar for meals. Occasionally, she would mix up biscuits or cornbread for something different.

Even though Jack was only seven he cajoled and nursed his family with sips of water and broth. Gladys and Pa didn't let him touch the dirty linen, but he stayed in the sick room while they took care of the necessary jobs on the farm. Pa fed the livestock and chickens while Gladys attempted to stay on top of food preparation and dishes. They both fruitlessly scrubbed the floor with carbolic acid, and all three pairs of hands were red and raw from the constant use of hot water and disinfectants.

They slept when exhaustion overtook them and woke to pitiful moans and smells.

Ten days earlier, Ivy had come home to Leedey from Weatherford Teacher College with a bad headache and fever. Ma put her to bed thinking she'd caught a late summer flu. Within a few days Pa called Doc Seavey because Ivy's symptoms worsened with a cough and nosebleeds.

"I think it's typhoid," Doc said seriously. "You'll be fortunate to pull through this without loss. Listen carefully and I'll write down what you need to do. No one leaves the farm. You're quarantined and I'm sending a colored woman to help. She's . . ."

"No you ain't." Pa said emphatically pointing his finger at the Doctor and drawing closer, "I ain't havin' no such woman on my place."

Doc shook his head in disbelief, "She's had this and is a good worker. I'll bring her tomorrow when I come to inoculate the rest of you. Remember to boil everything. Don't dump the sick waste down the privy; dig a hole and keep it covered with lye and dirt. We don't want this to spread around the county. No one else has it, and I want to keep it that way."

"You must be deaf. No colored woman's comin' on my place to care for Ivy. We'll shift for ourselves," Pa jutted out his jaw and poked Doc in the chest. "Gladys is strong and can help her Ma. The boys and me will get what's left of a crop in."

"I don't care about your crop and I don't like you." Doc leveled his gaze and shifted his bag. He poked Pa right back, "Don't threaten me. You've never seen typhoid ravage a family and it's a woman killer with the amount of work that goes into nursing. You'll get it and it'll kill all of you."

Doc turned to the house where Ivy lay. "I don't want Gladys or the boys even in the house. They stay in the barn. Again, no one leaves. Mattie's going to have a powerful amount of work. Let me send help."

"Gladys will take care of us and the cookin'," Pa lowered his voice and ground a pebble with his boot. "Mattie will see to Ivy. And that's final."

"Your pride will be your destruction or, worse yet, your wife and children," Doc spat out the words.

Ma was not party to the conversation because she'd left to tend Ivy. Gladys kept Jack entertained on the porch, but she was listening. Doc turned towards the house and hollered, "Gladys, wash your hands all the time and keep the boys clean. I'll check back tomorrow."

Just then Clarence came from the privy, rubbed his eyes, and complained of a headache. Doc took one look and sent him to bed.

"Simmons, remember no one but Mattie tends to Ivy and Clarence. And start digging that pit."

He got into his Model T and drove down the bumpy, dusty farm road and stopped at the fence. He hung a big yellow quarantine sign that scared Gladys and Jack almost as much as the thought of inoculations.

The next morning, Doc came to the house and placed a clean white cloth on the kitchen table. He warned Gladys and Jack not to touch anything. He carefully placed screws, and glass syringes with four hollow needles and four small clamps in a pot of boiling water on the stove. After a minute he removed these with tongs he had wiped down with alcohol and placed them on the cloth. He then rinsed his hands in alcohol, and using the clamps, assembled the syringes and needles. The needles were long and fat. He explained to the children that it was important that they be sharp and not have burrs. He'd spent the previous evening sharpening them.

"No denying that an inoculation hurts, but at least the needle won't get stuck or pull. The needles are big so they don't break off in your skin," Doc explained to Gladys. Jack was outside throwing up in the dead rose bush. Gladys was afraid he might have typhoid, but Doc explained that vomiting or passing out was a common reaction to his needles.

The preparations fascinated Gladys. Doc told her about the nurses he had worked with and the uniforms they wore.

"Could I be a nurse?" she asked.

"Someday, maybe," Doc said. "It's hard work, but you're no stranger to that. Watch while I fill the syringes, and then go get Jack. We'll talk later."

Gladys held Jack on her lap while Doc inoculated him in his upper left arm. First, he swabbed Jack's arm with a piece of muslin and alcohol. When the needle pierced his skin Jack, let out a yelp and shut his eyes crying into Gladys's flat chest. Soon it was over, and when Doc presented him with a piece of ribbon hard candy, all was forgotten. Jack sucked happily and went to get Pa while Gladys rolled up her sleeve. The shot hurt and her eyes filled with tears, but she was fascinated that the contents of the syringe were now in her body.

"I ain't gettin' sick," she muttered to the empty syringe and gladly took her piece of candy.

"You want to help?" Doc asked. "It's good practice. Take the empty syringes, disassemble them, and put them in water and bring it to a gentle boil. I always disinfect the syringes after and then again before I use them."

Ma came into the kitchen and wearily sat down.

"Ma, how 'bout some tea?" Gladys said.

"I'd like that, and please make Doc and Pa a cup, too," Ma said. "I've missed sharin' our cup of tea in the mornin'."

"Me, too," Gladys said wistfully.

Doc quickly took care of Ma's shot, and then she finished her tea and went back upstairs. Jack came in with Pa. Gladys silently handed Pa his cup, and he poured the tea into the saucer to cool and slurped. His eyes were tired as he looked around the kitchen and he noticed Gladys taking a syringe from the boiling water.

He frowned and turned to Doc.

"I don't have much this year," Pa said.

"Let's worry about it later. Get your family back on their feet, and I'll be by every day to check."

Ma came down with typhoid two days after her shot. She failed quickly.

It seemed that Ivy might pull through, but one night her fever went sky high and she started playing piano on the sheets and singing through cracked lips about angels and the sweet by and by. She was gone by morning.

Ma died the day after. During the night, Jack climbed up into bed with her, and Pa found him at dawn fast asleep with his arms hugging Ma's neck. She was cold and gray but her lips were on his forehead. Pa carefully moved Jack and lay him down next to Gladys and went and held Mattie's hand. Clarence lay close by in a stupor; Pa started telling Mattie about his early life in Alabama. His broken voice woke Gladys and, as the early morning light streamed into the bedroom, she saw Ma had passed. She silently cried and sat in the doorway listening to Pa.

"I ain't never been straight with you Mattie," Pa said. "This is my last chance. I loved you from the moment I saw you. All I ever wanted was to make a home for you. I wasn't ever gonna tell you the truth, but I will now.

# CHAPTER FIVE | PA'S STORY

*1888*

"If we don't run now, we'll be stuck here for the winter and I ain't takin' another whippin'. Indian Territory is open," James said to his brother as he tucked his shirttail into his pants and then adjusted his suspenders. "And we got money set aside."

Pa was waiting in the barn when they came home from fishing that warm fall day and they had caught a creel of fish for supper. Pa had thrashed his sons even though they were near about grown, because the ten cows bellowed to be milked.

The boys looked enough alike to be twins. Mama Cleta suckled them as infants and loved them both as her own. James did not remember his own mother as she had died soon after he was born of childbed fever and Pa had never remarried.

"Ma will fret herself to death if we don't tell her," Joe said.

"You know Pa; he'll get it out of her. We can't," James said.

The boys brought the milk pails to their mother. They washed at the trough and came in for supper.

Pa and Mama Cleta lived as husband and wife and the family didn't put on pretense when no one else was there. Ma put cornbread, collard greens, ham, fried trout and sweet potato pie on the table. The family ate in silence; after the dishes were done, they sat on the porch and enjoyed the cool night breeze. Ma sewed on a quilt until it was too dark to see.

"Simmons," Ma said to Pa, "I aim to go to town sometime. I need some calico for a new dress and the boys are growin' like weeds and outta shirts. They'll pass their shirts to you from now on."

"Me and the boys were gonna mend the fence tomorrow to keep in the sow," Pa replied and stroked his chin. "Maybe since they're so grown they'll fix it themselves."

"Pa, how're we supposed to fix that fence?" James said aghast at the suggestion. "That ol' pig charges anytime she feels like it."

"She ain't caught ya yet," Pa said.

"We've been lucky. She's a demon, with devil eyes," Joe said.

"Maybe they ought to wait until you get back and can help," Mammy said.

"Nope," Pa said. "I don't wanna wait, keep a sharp eye out, boys."

"Stubborn fool," Ma murmured under her breath and gesturing to the two boys said, "Come over here and hug my neck."

They hugged her and walked to the hayloft. They preferred it to the house.

"We ain't runnin' till that fence is fixed, "Joe declared. "I ain't leavin' Ma to be gored."

In the moonlight James nodded in agreement. They climbed into the loft and nestled into the quilts and hay. Neither boy slept much that night. Their dreams were haunted with visions of yellow tusks and demons staring at them through narrow-slit eyes. Mama Cleta and Pa left before light the next morning clattering away in the old wagon. Town was six miles away; they expected to return after nightfall.

The brothers completed their morning chores and ate cornmeal mush with cream and honey. While finishing their coffee they discussed the day's work ahead.

"We gotta watch out for that ol' pig every moment. I'll dig with my back to the house and you dig with your back to the barn and we ought to be able to see her comin'," Joe said.

"Smell her comin'," James said. "We oughta take the rifle loaded and ready to shoot, but Pa'd nail our hides to the smokehouse, if we shot her."

"Law, there ain't another sow around here who litters 14 shoats at a time, even if she does eat three or four of 'em," Joe said, breaking up the hard dirt with a post hole digger.

The boys wrestled with the old broken posts. They made a mix of soil, water, and gravel, then poured and tamped it around each new post. Sweat stung their eyes and they frequently wiped their foreheads with matching red kerchiefs. Their hat brims were low to keep the sun out of their eyes.

They didn't notice the sow until she came bellowing out from behind the barn.

Both boys took off running towards the house, not looking back as they raced towards safety. Joe reached the house first and heard a scream. He looked back and saw the sow ripping into James.

"Beat her with your fists, I'm a comin'," he yelled and grabbed the gun from over the door. He ran and yelled, and then whacked at the sow with the blunt edge of the rifle. She dodged his blows and with one final swipe she gored James' inner thigh and fled to her refuge under the barn.

James lay unconscious in a pool of his own blood. His left thigh was flayed and gashed to the bone. Joe quickly ripped up his shirt and made a tourniquet to staunch the flow of blood. He pulled James up onto the shady porch and brought a quilt. Joe cleaned and dressed the wound and sat by him with the gun by his side. If that sow came back, he would shoot it.

All through the long afternoon he swatted flies, poured water on the dressing, and released and tightened the tourniquet so James had a hope of keeping his leg.

James stirred and Joe heard, "Water."

He brought a cool dipperful from the well and James took a long drink.

"How bad?" James asked.

"Bad. We ain't goin' anywhere anytime soon. I ain't leavin' you to run to the neighbors; we gotta wait for Ma and Pa."

"I don't know if I'll last."

"You gotta."

"Can't feel my leg, so thirsty."

Joe cradled his head in his lap and gave him drinks throughout the long evening and into the night. James was in and out of wakefulness. Joe told him stories about Indian Territory and the farm they'd share. He looked up at the Milky Way and prayed to God to help his brother.

Finally, he heard the crunch of wagon wheels in the yard.

# Chapter Six | Pa's Story in Town

*1888*

"Simmons, I have to take the leg now or he's going to die," Doc wiped his hands. "James is burning with fever and those red streaks mean the flesh is mortifying. He'd be dead now if Joe hadn't stopped the bleeding. Mammy and I'll handle this. Go on outside and wait."

Pa didn't say anything. On his insistence, they'd brought James to town. Ma had wanted him to ride for the doctor. Instead, she'd packed James in quilts and as the wagon jolted down the rutted road Ma did her best to ease his suffering with whiskey.

Seeing his brother ride away in the wagon near about killed Joe.

"Finish the chores," Pa had barked. "And walk to town when you're done."

Joe milked the cows, fed and watered the chickens and stock before running all the way to town and nearly beating Pa.

Seeing Joe, Ma hugged his neck and turned to Pa. "If you weren't so pig-headed you'd have listened to the boys in the first place. Now get outta the way 'cause I aim to boil every knife Doc's got. I ain't been James' Ma for seventeen years to see him die 'cause somethin' ain't clean."

Frowning Pa said, "Guess we'll see to the horses."

"Good idea and then why don't you see if there's a hangin' at the courthouse. Maybe your own if I'm lucky."

Despite the seriousness of the operation, Doc chuckled and went about his own preparations. Cleta was a good nurse. When folks were in pain, they weren't too particular that she was the illegitimate daughter of sharecroppers and had herself bore an illegitimate son. People in the small town might gossip, but no one objected much to her relationship with Johnson Simmons.

Orella, the mother of James, had died soon after his birth. It wasn't uncommon for men to visit the old slave quarters where the sharecroppers lived, and Johnson was no exception. He quit his visits after he married, but Cleta was already pregnant with Joe. Out of necessity and love, she raised both boys.

"Cleta, open every window. I'm taking the leg clear to the hip," Doc said. "It won't give him anything to walk with, but it's the only chance I have of saving his life."

"There was a powerful amount of blood on the quilts and porch," she said. "Do what you gotta do."

Tears streamed down her face as she poured alcohol over their hands and Doc handed her the bottle of chloroform and the dropper basket with a clean cloth to cover it.

"Give this to James one drop at a time. Cover his nose and we'll be working fast."

"I know Doc, I done this before."

Doc bent over James and thought of the carnage and bloody operating theaters of the Civil War. Every limb he cut off irrevocably changed the life of a man. So many young men and boys and so many dead. The faces of the maimed and dying still haunted him. The bandages and instruments he now used were sanitized, but back then they reused everything without bothering to clean between patients. Most of the men died of infection anyway. He'd doctored for the South, but he would not fight for a way of life he hated.

He could take a limb in five minutes. The surgery wasn't pretty, but it was effective and men who lost a leg low enough could ambulate with a wooden one. James wouldn't be so fortunate. Doc knew he most likely would survive the operation, but not the recovery. He reapplied the tourniquet as far up on the leg as he could and tightened it.

He picked up the scalpel, "All right, start dripping."

Cleta nodded and applied the chloroform.

Doc waited and then quickly made a deep cut above the wound and switched to the bone saw. It was over in less than ten minutes.

Doc looked at Cleta. She was still as a statue with her eyes glued to the rising and falling of James' chest.

"I want him to sleep, so give him enough to slow his breathing even more. Let's get this wound packed with garlic and honey and then go find Simmons and Joe."

Joe kicked the dirt as he and Pa walked out of the livery and towards Main Street. The sun was coming up and a few horses were tied to a hitching post. They passed the empty schoolhouse painted white and smelling of pine. James told Joe that if you didn't talk to yourself as you ciphered and read the teacher would give you a whipping. Since he wasn't welcome, he stayed home and helped Pa during the day. James taught him what he learned at night and as a result Joe knew as much as his brother. James borrowed books from the school library for Joe to read such as Ivahoe, The Illiad, Robinson Crusoe and Gulliver's Travels. He in turn told James about the stories when they plowed the fields or as they lay in the hayloft.

The house was small, and Pa was harsh. The snorts and soft breathing of the animals set better than the sounds Pa and Ma made sometimes. Ma kept them well supplied with quilts so they were snug even in the cold winter.

As they walked along, Pa suddenly grabbed Joe's collar and thrust him in an alleyway. His face was purple with rage. He flung Joe against the wall and started punching and kicking him. Joe fell down against the store and shielded himself as best he could.

Pa suddenly stopped and looked to the sky. "You took the wrong leg. Take this boy's leg and let my son keep his."

Joe uncovered his face. It hurt to breathe, and his heart thumped as if to burst. He already blamed himself, but the words Pa uttered cut him.

"I'm sorry."

His humility took the anger from Pa, but he didn't offer a hand to help him stand. He just cursed softly and hit his fist into his open palm. As Joe struggled to right himself, Pa said, "Go clean up while I get us somethin' to eat."

Joe spat blood and shuffled to the oblong horse trough and dunked his head. He felt like climbing in and dunking his whole body. He took deep gulps of water. Somehow, he and James were still going to Indian Territory even if he had to push him all the way in a wheelbarrow. Ma was going, too.

Because of his injuries, he walked to the back door of the diner. He looked in and saw Pa sitting down and eating bacon and eggs. A lady come and handed him a sandwich wrapped in waxed paper and a glass of lemonade. He noticed his glass had a big chip in the rim.

"Simmons said to give this to you. Law boy, what happened? Get kicked by a horse?"

"No Ma'am."

He found a shady spot underneath a big tree and leaned against the trunk. The leaves were just beginning to turn yellow. The ground was a carpet of green grass and brown dirt. The lemonade stung his mouth, but he savored the sweet cold taste. He couldn't see out of one eye and his ears were ringing. The egg sandwich was easy to chew. He felt his teeth with his tongue. They were still all there, although a few seemed loose. He knew they would tighten up in a few days. He was beginning to relax and doze when a shadow blocked the sunlight.

"Get up. James is out of surgery."

By the time Joe and Pa arrived at Doc's, Joe's eyes were slits and his face nauseating shades of deep purple and blue. His nose dripped blood and was crooked. He limped towards his Ma who had hurried back.

She took one look at her boy and punched Simmons knocking him down.

"You no good bastard," she seethed.

She yelled, "Doc, come see Joe. Simmons beat him within an inch of his life."

Doc wearily came to the front room. He glared at Simmons and guided Joe to the exam room and sat him down. Going to the doorway he gave instructions.

"Simmons, get off the floor and make sure James is breathing. Let me know if anything changes. Cleta, draw a fresh bucket and make some lemonade. Add lots of sugar and a handful of salt for the boys."

He shut the door and set to work on James. He quickly assessed that besides the injuries to his face he had two cracked ribs and a bruised kidney. Joe dropped his overalls and his legs were covered in bruises and broken skin.

"Why didn't you fight back?"

"I only thought about protectin' my teeth."

"Still, this is a powerful beating."

Tears escaped Joe's swollen eyes. "To him, I'm just a boy not a son. He said God made a mistake."

Doc patted his shoulder and gave him his handkerchief. "Compose yourself and never let that son of a bitch see you cry. Soon as I'm done wrapping your ribs, I want you to get in bed next to your brother. Your Ma is gonna bring you in some lemonade and medicine."

Doc finished and found Cleta. He handed her a small bottle of laudanum. "Put a dropperful in Joe's lemonade. He'll rest."

"Okay. Tell Johnson to stay away from my boys. I'll tend 'em."

Doc took two glasses of lemonade and went to the front porch where Johnson Simmons sat slowly rocking in a wicker chair. Doc skirted the potted geraniums and pulled his own chair opposite him. He took a pistol and laid it on the table.

"Doc, my son gonna make it?"

"Which son, Simmons?"

"You know which one."

"Unfortunately, I do and I don't know the answer. Joe did a good job with the tourniquet, but James lost a lot of blood.

He's young and strong and where there's life there's hope." Doc swallowed. "What happened between you and Joe?"

"He wasn't lookin' out for James. I warned them about that sow and he shoulda kept a sharper lookout."

"It was an accident and Joe's not to blame. You have two sons and you better start praying that both boys pull through. He saved James' life. Be grateful. Those boys are men. Make peace while you can."

"What did he tell you? That lazy son of a bitch got no reason to involve you in our affairs. If James dies, I'll kill him, hell I'll kill him now." Simmons spat and stood up.

Doc picked up the pistol and pointed it at Simmons' heart.

"Sit down. You lay another hand on Joe and I'll shoot you. Ignorance and pride are why both your sons are in such a sorry state. I've patched up two Simmons men today, don't make it three."

"You listen to what he says." Cleta hollered through the open window. "I despise you and I ain't nothin' but what you made me be. Don't come in this house. I ain't got this butcher knife for nothin'."

Temporarily defeated Simmons sat down, "Got any whiskey?"

Cleta snorted, "Stay put, Doc. I know where you keep it. Maybe if he gets good and drunk you can knock sense into his head. I don't want him sneakin' in this sick room."

Cleta stomped out with a bottle and two glasses. She went back and settled her bony body in the middle space between her two sons, one of her body and both of her heart. As twilight deepened the frogs and locusts joined the two voices out on the porch. She wrapped an arm around each boy and felt the rise and fall of their breathing. She let her mind wander back through the years. She wished for one day of just her and her two baby boys. She sang their special lullaby while the butcher knife lay between her breasts.

44

*Rock-a-bye, rock-a-bye*
*Rock-a-bye, my baby.*
*Go to sleep, go to sleep*
*Go to sleep, my baby.*

# Chapter Seven | Leaving Time

*Fall 1888*

James lay in the front room next to the window. He looked at the desolate farmyard and watched the chickens searching for bugs. In the distance he saw the tree line. He knew he would never see Indian Territory. It was so hard to stay awake and not let the blackness and comfort of death take him. He had one last job to do before he could rest with the angels and meet his mama. Joe's survival depended upon him.

His leg was gone, and the pallor of his face matched the bleached bed sheets. He had insisted that his folks bring him home after the operation even though the bumpy wagon ride had been agony.

The cloudy sunset doused the room in vivid hues of orange, purple, and pink. Joe napped in a chair next to the bed and woke with a start when James grabbed his hand.

In a voice barely above a whisper he said, "Joe, I need you to listen 'cause I ain't got much time left."

Joe shook his head and rubbed his eyes. "What did you say?"

"I said listen to me," James grasped his hand harder and spoke louder. "Doc told Pa and Ma that there's no hope. You gotta go now because Pa won't start lookin' for you until after I'm gone."

Surprised Joe said, "James you're talkin' crazy. You just need time and then we'll go together, like we planned."

With his heart jumping in his chest, James raised himself on one elbow and told him, "I'm dyin'. I've looked at you every day for as long as I remember. And you're gonna go to the Territory. Take my name and papers and the money we've saved. You ain't stayin' and watchin' me die."

"I can't do it," Joe choked back tears. "You and Ma's all I got."

Ma brought in a freshly drawn pitcher of water from the well. She poured a glass and helped James by supporting his back and held the glass to his mouth. James tried to drink but most of the water ran down the towel around his neck. Ma laid him down and applied an ointment of camphor and duck grease to his dry and chapped lips. They were starting to lose their color and she knew he wouldn't last the night.

Ma wiped her eyes with her apron and looked at Joe. "Listen to your brother. Don't think, just go. I need to know one of you survives. My heart can't take much more."

"But, Ma, I can't go and leave you and James!"

"You gotta go and make somethin' of yourself! There's nothin' here but sadness." She kissed Joe and pushed him away. "Now move! He'll think you went to bed in the barn. Your food sack's packed and in the kitchen."

Looking between the two of them, Joe knew he was beat. He kissed Ma and his brother's hot forehead and left the room. He slipped the packet of food in his knapsack, put on Pa's old coat, and grabbed the papers, money, and bedroll from the barn. Walking to the edge of the farm he looked back and thought of the dreams they had made, that lay like the dust at his feet.

He'd walk and hide in creeks and ravines until he came to country where no one would recognize him. Then, hopping a train he would ride and buy a decent horse, saddle and gear; maybe when he got to Texas, he could work on one of the big cattle ranches near Abilene or cowboy on the American Trail.

His heart was sore. His brother would soon be dead, and Ma was sacrificing herself and an extra set of hands by sending him away. He didn't know what Pa would do once he realized he was gone and no one was left to work the farm. Joe felt like a yellow-livered coward for leaving Ma to face him alone.

"I'll send for her," he said to himself.

As the twilight deepened, he broke into a trot, spat on the ground and said, "I'll never forgive or forget you, Johnson Simmons. "

Suddenly he stopped. From the inner front pocket of the coat, he found his handwritten birth certificate that certified he was illegitimate. Carefully lighting one of his matches he put flame to the paper and burnt his identity. Reaching in again, he withdrew his brother's certificate and studied the particulars:

*Certificate of Birth, Coffeyville, Alabama*
*April 1, 1871*
*Born to- Orella Goodrum Simmons and Johnson W. Simmons*
*Sex - male*
*Race - white*
*Legitimate - yes*
*Weight - 9 pounds*
*Length - 21 inches*
*Name – James Lee Simmons*
*Witnesses – Dr. Randolph Butler, Cleta Simmons*

"James is now who I am," and he disappeared into the night.

Pa's eyes lost their faraway look as he looked down at his dead wife. He closed her eyes and his shoulders shook with grief. Broken, he continued, "Mattie this is what I've never had the guts to tell you."

Gladys overhearing the story walked over and stood by her Pa. She put her arms around his neck, something she'd never done before.

"Mattie?" Pa asked.

"No Pa. It's me Gladys," she said.

His eyes opened. "You remind me that I left my ma behind in Alabama when she needed me most. She had the same frost eyes as you."

Unwrapping her arms from his neck he left the room.

Gladys climbed up in bed next to her mama and cried.

# Chapter Eight | Tea at the Cemetery

*1923*

The small crowd stood on a rise of rust colored earth at Shirley Cemetery. It was a bitterly cold November day; gray, cloudy, and snow threatened. Stands of trees were about blown bare by the wind. Orange, yellow, and brown leaves circled the mourners in a somber dance. The town's people came to comfort the family and pay their respects to Mattie, Ivy, and Clarence. Typhoid took them within a day of each other.

Because of the weather the service was short, and a hot meal awaited everyone at the Simmons' home place. Daisy and Bud had arrived earlier in the week and helped Gladys, Pa and Jack scrub the house. It seemed to Gladys the smell of dying was finally gone.

She couldn't think of the last month and all the death without finding it hard to swallow. No matter how much she brushed her teeth, her tongue felt like it was growing brown fur and the taste of sick was always in her mouth. Gargling with peroxide didn't help. Gladys felt the smell of dirty laundry and flies on her and, consequently, took a sponge bath three or four times a day.

She knew she was safe because of the inoculation, but she still had nightmares about the messy death typhoid caused. Why had she been spared when Mama was so needed?

She missed Clarence. He was closest to her in age, and they had played and talked together in the barn. They often shared a stick of candy between them. The walk to school this winter would be lonesome.

She wouldn't miss Ivy, much. Even after Daisy married and moved to Oklahoma City, Ivy still ignored her. Gladys had hoped, before Ivy went to teacher college, they might share secrets, but Ivy had turned her back to her and pretended to sleep when she tried to talk.

Gladys missed Ma with an ache about to swallow her up.

"Ashes to ashes and dust to dust, the Lord giveth and the Lord taketh away, blest be the name of the Lord," the preacher intoned as he committed the bodies to the three open graves.

Pa came forward and threw shovelfuls of red clay on the wood caskets already lowered in the ground and handed the shovel to Bud, who did the same. Daisy shoveled after Bud and collapsed in a fit of weeping. Pa held her up and tried to give the shovel to Gladys. Gladys ignored him, picked up a fistful of dirt and attempted to release it over the coffin of Ma, but her fingers wouldn't open. Bud came over and gently pried her hand open and the dirt fell. Bud held Jack who released a tiny fistful of dirt also.

Bud took Gladys by the shoulder and steered her to the edge of the cemetery, and they sat down on a bench. They watched the town's people take their turns filling the grave and murmur words of comfort to Pa and Daisy. Jack toddled over and played in the dirt at their feet.

A wrought iron fence and a sign in curly script set apart the cemetery from the surrounding prairie and schoolhouse. The mourners left the desolate place by the gate under the Shirley Cemetery sign. The small settlement contained three or four small cemeteries. Folks didn't have to travel far to mourn and visit their dead.

After everyone was gone, Gladys, Jack and Bud walked over to the graves and peered down. The three coffins were only partially covered with dirt.

"Do you think we ought to finish fillin' in the holes? They might get cold," Gladys said.

"Let's make sure their coffins are covered and then Pa and I'll finish tomorrow," Bud said. He handed her the shovel, but Gladys fell to her knees and started pushing dirt from the side of Ma's grave. Jack clumsily dropped dirt in Ma's grave a handful at a time.

Bud worked on the other two graves. Tearing up, Gladys stood and said, "As long as you promise to finish tomorrow, I think Ma will be okay tonight."

Bud sensing her despair said, "Anything I can do, Bit?"

"Naw," Gladys said in a clogged voice. "Just tell Pa I'm gonna sit awhile with Ma. I ain't ready to go back. I ain't hungry and I don't want to feed no one. I ain't listenin' to anybody tellin' me to eat or wash dishes, especially Daisy."

"She's been on a bit of a toot," Bud smiled. "Take your time. I'll handle Pa and all them. People ain't goin' nowhere as long as there's food to eat and sympathy to give out.

"Thanks Bud," Gladys said. "I wanna say good-bye, one more time."

"I wish I could've been here sooner to lighten your load," Bud said taking off his overcoat and buttoning it over her thin frame. He gave her a hug, picked up Jack, and walked down the hill to the crowd gathering at the farm.

Gladys looked around at the brown and red hills. She gazed at the familiar landscape of her childhood. She took in the small gathering of people, buggies and a few cars that were parked in her family's farmyard.

She walked through the rows of graves and noticed how many women and infants were buried. Ma had turned forty last month and had buried two young children before Gladys was born. Leva Alice had died of croup and Alfred Lee had lived only a couple of hours.

Five graves now marked the Simmons family plot and Gladys wondered who would be number six.

The Klem family donated the land for the cemetery from their section. They too had buried several of their children. Most of the graves had rocks piled on top of them and the cemetery consisted of brown grass and weeds.

She walked alongside the wrought iron fence and stopped in back of the big concrete marker for the Simmons family plot. She took a small basket and sat down by Ma's grave. Gladys set up a tea party. From a small canning jar filled with milk, sugar and tea, she fixed two cups and placed ginger cookies on the rim of the saucers.

"Ma, I wanted us to have one last special time. I know your body's in that grave, but you always told me the spirit goes elsewhere. Maybe part of you is still here."

A trail of tears ran down her nose and taking a napkin, Gladys wiped her eyes and continued, "I heard Pa talk to you about Alabama. He hates me. What am I gonna do? I'm so scared."

Gladys drank her tea and the cold wind blew her hair into her eyes and mouth.

Fat raindrops started to fall. She pulled up the hood of Bud's coat, then opened the jar and poured the left-over tea on Ma's grave. The soft glow of oil lamps weakly lit the darkness through the windows of the farmhouses. The shadows lengthened and the rain came down harder.

"Daisy's probably gonna have kittens because I ain't there to help, Ma. She brought her baby but left her husband at home. Estelle didn't come with Bud. She's gotta stay in bed until her baby comes."

Gladys nibbled on another cookie and dropped the rest carefully in the open grave.

In the distance coyotes yipped. Gladys shivered in the cold and huddled next to the dirt piled up by Ma's grave. She knew the coyotes wouldn't hurt her, but still felt a little spooked.

She packed up her little basket and started sobbing, "I don't wanna be alone."

The wind died down and a warm soft breeze blew lightly threw her hair. It felt like Ma's fingers were fixing her hair with ribbons and bows. She relaxed and enjoyed the sensation.

"Ma?" Gladys whispered, "I knew you wouldn't leave me."

The warm breeze continued to blow. The wind bent the surrounding trees almost to the ground, but not where she sat.

She felt calm and peaceful and very sleepy. Stretching out in Bud's overcoat she lay down next to the open grave and pillowed her head with her hands.

She fell asleep dreaming about Ma. It was early summer, and they were chasing lightning bugs in the front yard. They walked down the pathway to the shady creek and Ma seemed to say, "I love you. Carry me in your heart and love Jack."

Gladys stretched out her hand in her sleep and Ma's fingertips seemed to touch hers.

She slept untroubled for the first time since everyone took sick.

Before long, Bud came looking for her. Gently picking her up, he carried her home and put her to bed in his old room. He kissed her on the forehead and said, "Sleep tight, Lil Bit," and slept on the floor beside her.

# Chapter Nine | Cooking for Threshers

1924

It was so hot. Gladys took Jack and they made their way past the brambles to the tree lined banks of the creek that ran through their western Oklahoma farm. She was mad at Pa because he volunteered her to cook for a neighbor's threshing crew.

Just once she would like to be asked to do something instead of being told.

"Jack, be careful now around the wild plum trees," she warned. "Yellow jackets love 'em as much as we do."

"Okay," Jack said through a mouthful of plums. The juice ran down his chin.

"We'll go swimmin' when you get sticky or attract too many hornets," Gladys said while her fingers plucked the small juicy fruit."

Jack nodded and picked plums off the small trees that grew wild.

The buzzing of the hornets and cicadas barely registered in her consciousness that late summer morning. The six-man threshing crew would eat at their home place; most likely Pa had walked over to the neighbors to make sure enough food was being provided to feed them two hot meals a day and a cold supper, if they wanted it. Goodness knows they had nothing to feed people. They lived on eggs, cornbread and milk. How was she going to manage with only Jack to help? Pa had no idea the amount of work it took to feed a crew.

She knew from helping Ma in past years that breakfast was expected at seven, after the men had worked a couple of hours. She chewed her lip and thought about a menu. Gladys wished Ma were here because she wasn't comfortable being in charge.

Her hands flew through the branches and the purple plums softly plunked in the bucket she held in the crook of her arm. She popped one in her mouth and spit out the seed.

I hope he brings home a ham she thought to herself. It'll be good fried with eggs in the morning, and I can use it to flavor green beans for dinner. I'll use some plums and make pies tonight.

Jack came over with two full pails of fruit and helped her finish picking. They jumped in the creek, and splashed and swam in the slow-moving water. Then hiked up to the rutted dirt road just as Pa and their neighbor came rumbling down in a wagon.

"Hop in kids," Mr. Carlton sang out. "We're just takin' this load to your place. I appreciate you cookin' for me, Gladys. Look over what's back there and let me know if you think it's enough."

Gladys and Jack climbed in the back. She saw a crate of chickens, ham, baskets of green beans, a sack of flour, salt, sugar, cornmeal, and a crock of bacon grease. She glanced over the bed of the wagon and spied tomatoes, onions, lettuce and dishes in boxes.

"I'm sure I'll manage," she told him. "Thank you."

"My Gerva is stayin' in town with her ma until this baby comes. She's swelled up bigger than a toad and Dr. Seavey is checkin' on her every day." He offered Pa a chaw of tobacco. "You folks are gettin' us outta of a jam. I'm gonna need this crop and I'm thankful that prices are holdin' this year. I'm owin' the doctor already."

"I know all about owin' the doctor," Pa said adjusting his hat and taking a pinch from the offered pouch.

The fields surrounding Pa's were ripe with wheat, but his fields lay barren with brown stubble.

Mr. Carlton looked at the desolate farm and said, "You folks have gone through a rough time. Simmons, you and your team would be welcome tomorrow haulin' shocks to the barn."

"The machine binds the wheat into shocks, too?" Jack asked as the team plodded along.

"The machine cuts, binds, and spits the shocks out along with the stubble." Mr. Carlton said. "It does everythin' but drive the team."

"Seems like a wonder," Gladys said.

"It's a wonderful time," Mr. Carlton kept on, "things are changin' everywhere. Someday I bet we all own cars, tractors, and other amazin' machines and these two mules of mine won't be needed anymore."

They made the turn into the farmyard. The wagon stopped in front of the house.

"I'll feed you good, I promise," Gladys said and she and Jack jumped off. She grabbed the peaches and handed them to Jack, took the ham, and went into the house.

The men and Jack unloaded the wagon, and when they were done Mr. Carlton said he'd run into town to see his wife.

With a stubby pencil on the back of an envelope, Gladys scribbled a menu and took it over to Pa.

*Breakfast — sausage, eggs, fried potatoes, biscuits, gravy, coffee, jam, butter, cream and sugar*

*Dinner — fried chicken, potatoes and green beans, gravy, corn bread, tomato and cucumber salad, baked beans, plum and peach cobbler*

*Morning and late afternoon — ginger water and bread-and-butter sandwiches (Jack take to fields)*

*Supper — leftovers, ham sandwiches, and peanut butter cookies*

"Pa, would your wring the chickens' heads tonight?" Gladys asked. "I'll scald and pluck 'em after supper and then make pies."

"This food looks all right," Pa said checking the menu. "How many chickens? Make enough because I don't want you shamin' me 'cause we run out of somethin'."

"Four," Gladys said, flipping through Ma's recipe book.

Gladys got up before five the next morning and kindled the coals and added wood to the stove. She needed a hot fire for the biscuits. Counting her family and Mr. Carlton, she would be cooking for ten people. She thought about last year when the threshers came to their farm and all she did was set the table and run ginger water and bread-and-butter sandwiches to the fields. A tear escaped and she quickly wiped it from her face.

Crying won't help me none, now she thought.

"Help me Mama, and you too, Jesus," she prayed as she rolled out the biscuit dough. She had gotten in the habit of praying to both. Praying to Mama first made Jesus more real.

She fried up the sausage and eggs. Jack set the table and, when the biscuits were nearly done, he called the men. While the men ate she washed dishes.

At midmorning she took a break. Jack was out in the fields delivering ginger water to the thirsty workers.

So far so good she thought as she sipped her cold tea. "I only gotta do this the rest of today and tomorrow and then they're off to the next farm."

She looked at the baked beans and then put bacon grease in the fry pans. She dredged the pieces of chicken in a mixture of flour, salt, and pepper, and placed them in the hot fat, being careful not to crowd the pan or the chicken would not brown correctly.

Delicious smells soon filled the kitchen and she lost herself in the bustle of cooking noon dinner.

During dinner Gladys knew she was in for it because the gravy ran out. She'd made a whole skillet full, but the men dumped it on chicken, green beans, potatoes, corn bread, every-thing. By the time the gravy bowl got to Pa, there was hardly a scraping left.

"Come here, girl," Pa snarled, his face twisted in anger as he slapped her on the cheek. Her head twisted almost causing her to drop the load of dirty dishes she was carrying. "What did I tell you 'bout shamin' me?"

He had sent Jack with the men after dessert and coffee. They were all sprawled out resting and rocking on the cool porch and under the trees before going to the fields.

"Pa, I have chicken left and plenty of cornbread. No one went away hungry." Gladys said in a steady voice and defiantly looked him in the eyes. She managed to plop the pile of dishes in the sink full of soapy water.

"Don't matter, lean over," he said.

"You can beat me blue, but it ain't fair." She pulled away and ran to the pie cupboard using one of the doors as a shield. She glared at him, "I did my best."

"Fair don't matter." His belt whistled as he pulled it from around his waist. It snapped shut the door of the cupboard. He again raised the belt over his head and it cut her hands and neck. She ran to the corner and tried to protect her face from the stinging blows. Turning her back to him, he beat her. Gladys whimpered but refused to cry out.

Suddenly the blows stopped. Gladys raised her face and saw Mr. Carlton holding Pa's arm. He said, "Simmons, Gladys did a fine job and I'm beholden to her. I need you in the field."

Pa's arm fell and he left. Mr. Carlton helped Gladys up off the floor and onto a chair. He brought her a glass of water and brought a small quilt from the living room and draped it over her to quiet her shivering as she sobbed softly.

"I'll send Jack in."

Gladys looked up at him and pleaded, "Please don't tell no one else."

"I won't."

Gladys slid to the floor and crawled to the corner and cried. All the misery and sorrow she'd bottled up since Ma got sick and died tumbled out of her. For almost a year she'd run the house and taken care of Pa and Jack. She was plumb tired of his whippings and lack of gratitude.

Jack came running.

"Oh my, what did he do?" Dashing to the pump, he drew cold water from the depths of the earth. He offered another cup of cold water to his sister and placed wet clean rags over the welts on her face, arms and back

"I hate him," Jack fiercely said. He brought a pillow and placed it under her head and the quilt over her body. Sitting on the floor, he sang to her softly like she did so often for him when he missed Ma. He patted her arm in a spot that didn't hurt, and kept the rags wet.

"That's nice Jack," she said after her cries gave way to hiccups. Soon she breathed slowly.

"You rest, Sister. I'll clean up and take care of things."

Jack finished the dishes and filled the jugs with cold water from the pump. He sliced and buttered bread and made a stack of sandwiches. He placed the yoke across his shoulders, picked up the basket of sandwiches and put peaches in the basket, also. He kicked the screen door open and trudged across Pa's section to where the neighboring field began. He nodded to Mr. Carlton and placed the basket and water in the shade of a tree. Mr. Carlton came over and talked to Jack before whistling for the workers.

Gladys was awake when he came back. She'd changed clothes and was lying on the porch swing.

"You took care of everythin' good. Would you mind settin' out supper tonight? I'm gonna hide in the cellar."

"Mr. Carlton said to not worry about tonight, and make breakfast simple. He told Pa if he beat you again, he'd make sure the Sheriff put him in jail."

Gladys didn't answer him. She rocked slowly with her eyes closed.

Jack filled up the watering pail and pinched the heads off dead geraniums. He sprinkled the surviving flowers with water.

Opening one swollen eye, Gladys said, "Whatcha doin'? Ain't they all dead?"

"I don't think so. Ma sure loved to grow things. I keep thinkin' with enough water and pinchin', the flowers might come back."

"I hope so. Ma always told me some plants, like people, need a little longer to bloom, just don't pinch too hard."

"Okay," Jack said. "I'll remember."

# CHAPTER TEN | DEAD HOPES

*February 1924*

"Gladys," Pa called as he drove the worn wagon into the yard.

Gladys and Jack stopped feeding the chickens by the side of the house and ran to see him.

"Come here and get this trunk. "

Pa continued but didn't look at her. "I phoned Bud in town and fixed things so you're gonna cook at the Katy. With the baby and all, they need help."

"I'm leavin'?" she asked.

"Don't fuss. We're all leavin'. Me and Jack is going to live with Daisy, and she don't have room for you. I had to mortgage the farm to pay the bills."

After two years, Pa still owed the doctor and the funeral home. Gladys would never forget when Ivy came home early from Weatherford Teacher College, ailing. Later Clarence felt poorly with a high fever and headache. Mama nursed them both and never let Gladys or Jack in the sick room. Then she became ill. Providence and Dr. Seavey couldn't save them. Ivy succumbed first, then Ma and Clarence a day later. Gladys, Pa and even Jack had worked day and night taking care of everybody.

It was a record-breaking year for broom corn and wheat in Leedey. Pa continued to hire himself and Jack out through harvest. After Pa whipped her so hard, Gladys stayed home and quit school and Jack never started. No one cared to check. Farm work took precedence over learning.

She stumbled out of bed at noon, not bothering to change clothes or comb her hair. She did enough chores to escape a whipping and cooked sufficient dinner to see them through to the next day. Gladys quit caring about anybody but Jack. Pa was seldom home and it was a relief.

She and Jack lugged the trunk up the stairs and into her room. She opened it and they peered at the cavernous inside.

"Golly what are you gonna put inside of it?" Jack asked as he stepped in and sat down.

"Hopefully, you." She said and lifted him out. "I dunno. I don't have many clothes."

They heard Pa come up the steps and knock the dirt off his boots before coming into the front room. They came down the stairs and watched him sit down and rub his head.

"I want you to take what's left of your mama's effects and anything else you want out of the house. I don't want strangers going through our things. Wash and pack for I ain't sendin' you to Bud's dirty. Train leaves at nine in the mornin'."

"You want me to pack the churn? Can Jack go with me?"

"No he stays with me. I won't have you babyin' him and turnin' him into a sissy. What you don't take, I'm burnin'."

Gladys sat down with a plop by the window and knew it was useless to argue. She turned and looked at the farmyard and all she saw was lonesome. The windmill creaked as it pumped water into the stock pond, but there was only one milk cow left. Pa sold the others to pay bills. His crops of broomcorn and wheat were dry and withered by the wind that blew over the western Oklahoma prairie. The once thriving family farm was now desolate and empty. Ma had always kept busy feeding chickens, tending the kitchen garden or fussing at Clarence or Jack. This place was all Gladys knew. Now with Ma and the others gone she was not sorry to leave, but she hated to leave Jack.

Pa left and went to the barn.

Jack cried beside her.

"Hush Jack. I'll think of another way for us to be together. You know Pa will lick us both if you cry."

Pa came out of the barn and called, "Jack, muck out the stalls. It'll give you somethin' to do and be one less thing for that banker to talk about when he takes over."

Wearily the two children got up. Gladys finished feeding the chickens while Jack kept busy in the barn.

Pa's gruffness now extended to Jack as well. Any charitableness he once possessed now lay in the grave with his wife and other children.

Her thoughts tumbled in her head as she hurried to fill the big wash pot with water from the pump at the sink and placed it on the stove. While the water heated, she separated her clothes, and Pa and Jack's. When the water was hot, she dumped it into the wringer washer tub along with soap and the whites. She stirred the clothes with a long wash stick and occasionally fished an article out to give it a good scrub on her wash board.

She fed the soggy mess through the wringer on the back of the machine and placed the clean clothes in a wicker basket. The dirty water ran through a hose hooked to the bottom of the tub into the garden. She filled the tub with fresh water and then dumped the clean clothes and swished them with the stick, before running them through the wringer again. Finally, she hung them out to dry and repeated the process with the darker clothes.

Gladys was not surprised that Pa sent her to live with Bud. Even as a child, Bud always looked out for her. After he married Estelle and quit the rodeo, they opened a restaurant in Elk City.

Gladys did not know Estelle, but she seemed kind. Bud's family all lived in the one room at back of the diner. Gladys figured she would sleep on a cot in the kitchen. She wouldn't have minded sharing the kitchen with Jack. The Katy Coffee Shop took its name from one of the railroads that ran through Elk City.

Food. With all the sickness and sadness Gladys and her family had lived on eggs, milk, whatever fruits and vegetables Jack could scavenge from the garden or wild, and cornbread. She was longing for good things to eat again. She knew when fried chicken was done by the way it smelled. As she scrubbed the clothes, she thought about ham steak with green beans, new potatoes, and creamy red-eye gravy made from the crust left in the bottom of the fry pan. Jack said her pancakes were the best. Her mouth watered as she thought about a stack dripping with butter and molasses.

Gladys spent the afternoon scrubbing clothes and dreaming about the food she would cook and eat at the Katy. She would have to stay up late ironing and then pack her trunk when everything was clean and fresh. She would bathe later that night.

"If only Jack could come, I believe I might be happy," she said to herself.

They ate milk and cornbread and some onions gleaned from the garden for supper that night. Gladys asked Pa. "When am I gonna see Jack, again?"

Pa cleared his throat and left the table.

"I'll come and see you Gladys," Jack said.

"I know, but you're only eight and it's over 100 miles."

"Will Mama be at Daisy's house?"

"Jack, you know Mama's in heaven."

"Can I walk to heaven?"

"No you can't walk to heaven. You die to get there. When you go to bed, just pray to Jesus and ask him to say 'Hey' to Mama. That's what I do. Then forget about everything and go to sleep."

"I miss Mama."

Gladys got up and started stacking the plates.

"I said, 'I miss Mama!'"

"I know," Gladys said. "I miss Mama, and Clarence, but we can't bring them back. I'm sure they miss us. Now, bring me the rest of those dishes and if you're good maybe we can play some checkers before bed."

On the porch Pa sat, rocking in a chair, with a board on his lap. He was playing Ol' Sol with a deck of cards by the glow of the lamplight. He listened to the voices of his children as they talked and argued over their checker game. Tears streamed down his cheeks; he thought about all he wanted to say to his family, not just to the ones living, but those in the ground, including his brother and Ma buried in Alabama. He wanted to explain why he had to give up; his heart could not take anymore. He was broken. The years stretched empty before him, without a wife, farm or hope. His dreams were dead and all he could do was wait.

# CHAPTER ELEVEN | A NEW START

*1924*

Jack held on tightly to Gladys' hand as the big black locomotive clanged and shuddered its way into the station. The air was smoky around them and the smell of soot tickled their noses. Leedey was a quick stop and Gladys dropped Jack's hand and climbed aboard and found a window seat. She waved at Jack and looked hard at Pa who sat in the wagon. She tentatively waved good bye and he nodded his head at her as the train left the station.

The ride to Elk City took less than an hour even with a couple of stops. In a few days Pa and Jack would leave the farm and take the train to Oklahoma City to start their new life.

Gladys hadn't been hungry when she left the farm that morning. Jack had slipped her butter sandwiches and an apple when he gave her a hug. She didn't know how to live without him. He'd always been her baby to take care of. If only Pa would've let him come with her, she would've taken care of him.

She stared out the window and ate her apple. The fields lay empty except for shocks of wheat and hay. The wind had stripped the fruit trees bare except for a few stubborn leaves and windfalls. The birds flew south in the sky and the sun hid behind the clouds that held the season's first snowfall.

Gladys felt uncertain. A part of her was excited about living with Bud. She looked at her cracked and bleeding nails. Besides being rough from laundry and dishes, she picked at them and at a scab on top of her head, just to feel something. She knew she was still alive if her fingers or head hurt.

She looked at her coat. Ivy and Daisy had worn it before her. It was stained and the orange wool looked like a cat had died on it. At least it was warm. Her brown shoes were scuffed and too tight. They had once belonged to Clarence and her socks were a pair of Jack's. She hadn't cared how she looked the past couple of years but wished she didn't look so raggedy now.

"I'll save up and buy some clothes at Bud's," she muttered under her breath.

"Ma'am," said the Conductor. "I'll take your ticket."

Gladys silently handed it to him.

"We'll be another 30 minutes after we stop in Trail."

Gladys nodded and slightly smiled and wished he would go away.

She turned and gazed out the window and counted cows. Do cows get tired of standing in the field? How do the calves know which mama to go to?

Gladys noticed hundreds of crows gathered on the telephone wires. She wondered what made the wires swoop and if the perched birds could hear people talking through their toes. Did their tiny claws buzz with the voices of people?

She listened to the rhythmic clacking of the train. Her eyelids drooped and the next thing she knew, the train was slowing and the Conductor called out, "Elk City, next stop, Elk City."

Gladys glanced outside and saw Bud waving. She ran to the door, waited for the train to stop, and the Conductor put a stool down and helped her off the train. She ran to Bud and was enveloped in his overcoat with a big hug.

"I have a trunk."

"I'll fetch it after the lunch rush. Let's get home, Lil Bit," Bud said. "Estelle can't wait to meet you and she's got chili beans for lunch. Look left. Estelle and Lucille are wavin' at us."

Gladys looked where Bud was pointing and saw a pretty brown-haired lady holding a baby and hollering. They quickly walked the half block to the Katy Café.

"Gladys, Bud! Bud, we're swamped. Gladys, how do? We'll get acquainted later. Lucille, say hi to your aunt."

Lucille stretched out her arms towards Gladys and Estelle handed her over and gave Gladys a hug.

"Come on in. If you need to lie down, you and Lucille can rest on our bed in back. Bud and I have to take care of this rush."

Bud was already at the grill with an apron around his middle. Customers were calling their orders to him and he was cracking eggs and slapping meat on the grill.

Gladys held the baby and looked over the cheery diner full of customers and people standing up against the wall waiting to eat. She liked Estelle immediately. She loved babies and Lucille was sucking on two fingers and twirling her hair with the other.

"Pwetty," Lucille said. "You pwetty."

"Huh, she talks?" Gladys asked untangling herself from her niece. "I would be glad to help out, washin' dishes."

"Oh yes, she talks. Sometimes I think she was born jabbering." Estelle remarked and took her daughter back. "And you aren't shy about working. Bud told me as much."

Estelle gave her an apron and a hairnet. "I'm taking her next door for the neighbor lady to watch while she naps."

Bud said, "Bit, pick your poison, cookin' or counter?

Gladys hung her coat on a coat tree and looked around and noticed a group of dusty cowboys coming in for lunch. "Cookin', please. I ain't up to meetin' folks yet."

For the next two hours Bud filled drink orders and waited on customers. Estelle came back and ran between helping Gladys with the grill and catching the dishes up. The time passed swiftly and the rush was over. Estelle disappeared to retrieve Lucille, Bud left to get her trunk, and Gladys sat down on one of the red stools to wait. Bud returned and dished up chili beans and cut big hunks of cornbread. He poured hot tea into mugs and sat down with her.

"You did good today. Start eatin', 'cause you ain't nothin' but bones; Estelle and I aim to fill you out some."

It was all she could do, to not shovel the chili and buttery cornbread in her mouth. Bud noticed and cut her a bigger piece of cornbread and spooned more beans in her bowl. She took a gulp of the cooled tea and started eating again.

Estelle banged open the door with Lucille on her hip.

"Good. I hoped you all had started eating."

Bud got up to serve them. Estelle grabbed the highchair from the corner and set Lucille down. Bud mashed up beans for Lucille.

Lucille looked from her ma to her daddy and opened her mouth to holler. Bud made the most of the opportunity. Lucille scrunched up her face and spat the food back out.

"Wuck," she said.

Bud wiped his face and daughter's with a dish towel and removed her from her chair. "I got a bottle warmed up, Kid. You sit down with Gladys and I'll feed Baby Girl," Bud snagged the bottle from a pan of water on the stove and tested the temperature of the milk on his wrist. He stuck the bottle in Lucille's mouth and closed the bedroom door.

"She'll be out like nothing flat," Estelle said. "I can't thank you enough for helping. We've been in a world of hurt trying to feed everyone. Want some milk in your tea?"

"Yes please," Gladys said. "It was fun bein' busy."

"You're like me, you like to work hard. We'll have another rush in a couple of hours. But in the meantime, let's talk. We've got a rollaway in our bedroom that we'll bring out tonight." Estelle continued. "You can store your clothes in the little closet off the kitchen here. The privy is out back."

"I don't aim to be any trouble."

"Trouble? That's the last thing you are. You'll start school on Monday and I want to get you fixed for clothes. Let's take a peek in that trunk."

"I don't have much," Gladys said red-faced and opened it from the corner of the kitchen.       Estelle looked at the clean, but raggedy, sparse clothing wrapped around a teapot and two cups and saucers, an iron, and a family photograph. "Bud has this photo, too."

"Ma'am, I don't like to be beholden for clothes. I'll pay you back." Gladys said.

"Ma'am and beholden? What kind of talk is that? Let's get a few things straight," Estelle said. "We're going to take care of you and you're going to school. You can help us on Saturdays and during breaks, but you're going to get a high school education. Even though the law says you only have to go to school through eighth grade, we want more for you and Lucille."

"Oh no, I've already broken the law by not going to school in Leedey." Gladys said with a quiver in her voice, "Will I go to jail?"

"No, Honey, you will not go to jail. Now, we want you to dress as pretty as the other girls and have nice things. We aren't rich, but we've got enough and plenty to share. Let's hurry and finish up so we can shop. And no more Ma'am, call me Estelle."

Estelle looked at her with an expression that brooked no disagreement.

They ate rapidly and when Bud came back in the room, Gladys noticed Estelle nodded her head at him.

Bud sat down and started eating. "I guess you two have talked. Estelle, get what my sis needs and a few things she don't. Our credit is good anywhere, but I know you're partial to Anthony's."

"Yes I am," Estelle said. "C'mon Gladys, let's make hay while the sun's shining."

"Huh?" Gladys looked at her in confusion. "I thought we're goin' shoppin'."

"We are, Honey. That's just an expression meaning let's hurry up and go."

Anthony's Department Store was beautiful with a copper ceiling. It featured floor to ceiling picture windows that displayed mannequins wearing the latest shorter fashions from the big cities. Estelle moved like a whirlwind and Gladys tried on more dresses than she had ever seen in her life. She loved the dressing room with the velvet curtains. Estelle kept popping her head in to see how she looked. They both decided that the brown and blue plaid jumper was a good choice for school. Estelle picked out two blouses to go with it. Gladys tried on another outfit.

"The teal sweater set looks nice with your hair. You and Lucille are a pair of corn silk blondes. With this tan skirt, it'll be a nice outfit for church or a special occasion at school," Estelle said. "Try on this batch of dresses and pick two or three. Marjorie, she's going to need a slip and unmentionables. I'm gonna keep looking for what else you need. Hold on, that brassiere don't go on that way. I'll show you."

When Gladys emerged, the sales counter was piled with nightgowns, socks and a new comb and brush. She'd never seen so much stuff. Sensing how she felt, Estelle pulled her back in the dressing room to talk.

"Honey, I know this is a lot to take in, but you haven't had anything since your ma passed. Bud and I'll help you get used to things. You're in town now and life is different. None of the clothes you brought are worth saving. If you want, pay us back a little each week, but I prefer for this to be a gift. Instead of giving money to church the next couple of months, we'll just spend it on you. The Bible says if we don't take care of family, we're worse than heathens."

Gladys listened to her and nodded her head. She felt like crying with embarrassment and thankfulness. It had been so long since anyone had taken care of her, she didn't know how or what to say.

The train whistled in the distance and Estelle said, "I got to get back to Bud. You need a pair of sturdy, lace up shoes and Mary Janes for church and a coat."

"What are Mary Jane's?" Gladys said. "And I already have a coat."

"Shoes," Estelle said. "And your coat looks like fourteen people wore it before you did. I ain't sending you to school in something like that."

At that, Gladys laughed and then cried.

"On second thought, you're a bit wrung out; I think I'll stick around for a couple more minutes. We'll make it snappy."

The clerks pretended to be invisible while all this was happening. Estelle and Gladys found shoes and a beautiful blue wool coat.

"This coat will last for years. It's big, but you'll grow into it," Estelle said. "We'll get school supplies at the Five and Dime tomorrow. I hear that train whistling in town now and we got to get back."

"Estelle," Marjorie said. "Run on and we'll deliver all this by tonight. Nice to meet you Gladys, and welcome."

They left Anthony's and ran back to the Katy, barely beating the hungry trainmen and passengers.

That night Gladys sat on her bed by the warm grill wearing a blue flannel nightgown and looked at the pretty things piled around her. Earlier that evening, Estelle had trimmed her hair to get rid of the snarls and after a bath doctored her head and fingers with Methylate or monkey blood as Bud called it. The stuff tasted nasty and stung something fierce.

She could hear Bud and Estelle murmuring through their closed door. She felt the soft cotton of her slip and new panties. She had always worn a shift for an undergarment. Estelle told her she needn't wear the brassiere at night. "Estelle knows everything about woman stuff. I'm sure she'll help me rig something up for my monthlies," she said to herself.

Gladys looked around. The pilot light kept the kitchen warm. She carefully put her treasures back in the boxes they were delivered in but kept the beautiful blue coat in her arms. She turned off the overhead light and snuggled into her quilts and hugged the coat close to her. She didn't care if it was scratchy. It was the first coat she'd ever owned that was all hers.

She whispered her prayers, "I hope Jack is okay. Mama and Jesus keep him safe, and I'll send him some money for new clothes as soon as I can. I like it here. Amen."

# Chapter Twelve | Nerves

Through a sleep filled haze, Bud heard his daughter's voice.

"Is she sick?" Lucille said standing between Gladys and her ma in the kitchen of the cafe. "Why her 'frow up?"

In the bedroom Bud patted the bed trying to find his wife.

From the other room he heard, "Bud, come and grab Lucille!"

He reached for his pants at the foot of the bed. The door between the bedroom and café was closed, but enough light came through the bottom of the door that he saw that Lucille's trundle bed was empty.

Yawning he opened the door and said, "What's up, Kid?"

"'Bout time," Estelle grumbled. She was holding Gladys's hair back and wiping her face with a cloth. "Grab your daughter and bring Gladys a soda."

Bud snatched up his curious daughter who was peering into the basin on the floor.

"Lucille, what flavor will make Aunty Gladys feel better?"

Retching, Gladys shook her head that she didn't want anything.

"Make that soda water to calm her tummy," Estelle told Bud.

Speaking to Gladys, she smoothed the bed covers and said, "Honey, you just have the dry heaves now." Bud handed her a small glass.

Lucille wiggled out of Bud's arms and plopped on the bed. She handed Gladys her doll.

"Susie don't like it when you 'frow up,"

Gladys slowly sipped the soda water and hugged Lucille's doll.

"Nerves can do this to you," Bud said. Estelle got up and he took her seat. Estelle leaned against the counter with Lucille. Lucille yawned and Bud nodded to Estelle. "You and Baby Girl run on to bed and I'll sit with Sis until she feels better."

Estelle shut the door and Bud continued, "Clarence was one to throw up. Shovelin' manure used to make him gag so bad I'd finish whatever Pa had me doin' and go help him as quick as I could."

"I never knew that."

"I bet you didn't know Ma couldn't stand strong smells either." Bud said. "I always knew whenever she was carryin', because she couldn't bear the smell of fryin' meat or cooked cabbage. The big girls would take over for her until her stomach settled."

"Do you want a cracker or a real soda to drink?" Bud asked.

"No, I'm feelin' better now." Gladys said. "Do you remember when Ma was carryin' me?"

"I do," Bud said. "Ma lost the baby before you and we were all excited when she was carryin' again."

"Ma told me once about Alfred," Gladys replied and took a small sip. "She said he was so little and tiny and only lived for a few hours and she held him till he passed. I went with her sometimes to Shirley Cemetery to put flowers on his grave."

"Yes, he was a little one." Bud said. "I was a big kid in school, but every now and then I would go off and have a cry in the barn. I never knew him, but I still missed him."

"But then you came along and Ma said you were the biggest and prettiest baby ever. You had white curly hair that framed your face like a halo. You looked like a little owl peering around with your eyes bein' the color of a light blue sky."

"I hate my eyes and hair and lookin' different," Gladys said with a sigh. "Daisy and Ivy always made fun of me. They'd never helped me fix up. No one is gonna be my friend at school 'cause I'm so big and ugly."

Bud handed her a handkerchief and took the soda water from her. After she wiped her eyes and honked into the hanky, he took it back and patted her hand.

"Now listen, Bit. You gotta believe you've got just as much right to decent times and pretty things as anyone else and you ain't ugly."

Gladys motioned for the hanky again.

Taking a minute, she looked around the café. All the roller shades were down and the café curtains were closed. No one could see in. The café was cozy and she felt better.

For the last time she handed the hanky back to Bud and scrunched down to where she was under the covers. Only her face peeked out.

"I feel better Bud and I'll try."

Bud had noticed her looking around. "Okay, and maybe someday we'll have a real house and Jack can come."

"That'd be nice," Gladys said drowsily. "I think I can sleep."

"Nite Bit," Bud said as he turned off the light and went to bed.

# Chapter Thirteen | First Day of Eighth Grade

*1924*

Gladys and Bud walked together. If she wasn't so old, she would have held his hand. She couldn't eat the oatmeal Estelle made that morning. The brick school building loomed over Main Street and the big double doors looked like a mouth gobbling students up.

Bud, sensing her mood said, "Bit, you look nice in that dress and coat. We'll be waitin' to hear how things go."

He gave her a hug and they parted ways. Gladys took a deep breath, straightened her school bag and joined the rush of students. Being careful not to jostle anyone, she made her way inside. A gleaming staircase went up to the second and third floors. Students were everywhere. Glancing left, she saw a wooden door marked *Office* and entered. A bench hugged the wall. She took a seat, and waited to approach the front counter. A secretary was writing excuses for students who had been absent. A few stared, some smiled, but nobody said anything to her.

After everyone else had cleared out, she approached the front counter and said what Estelle had told her to say, "My name is Gladys Lee Simmons. I'm living with my brother and his wife, Bud and Estelle, at the Katy Café. I went to Liberty Center School in Leedey and I'm in the fifth reader."

"Good morning, Gladys Lee Simmons. I'm Miss Vaughn," the lady smiled at her and pointed to her name tag. "I've been expecting you. Bud hauls freight from the depot with my brother, Sterling, sometimes. Now do you have a report from Liberty School?"

Gladys fidgeted. "No Ma'am, I don't have no papers."

"How old are you?" Miss Vaughn tapped the counter with a pencil and looked at her like she was appraising a farm animal.

"I'll be thirteen in February," Gladys said and felt tears welling up in her eyes.

"Now, don't worry, we'll get you put to rights," Miss Vaughn said and handed her a tissue. "As a new student without records you'll need to take some examinations. There's a desk in the supply closet. It's quiet and private, so go have a seat and I'll get you started."

Miss Vaughn switched on a light and handed her two newly sharpened pencils and a stack of papers. Gladys went inside.

"Do as much as you can and tell me when you want a break. If you brought a lunch, you can eat in the office today or go outside. Good luck." Miss Vaughn said and kept the door open.

Gladys looked around at the paper, books, and supplies surrounding her and opened the test marked Arithmetic and looked over the first couple of problems.

$213 \times 14 =$
$428 \div 72 =$
*Write one million.*

After lunch she read with Mr. Shanks, the principal. She took the rest of her tests in his office and worked on American History.

After scoring her examinations, he told her it was time to meet her teacher. They walked the deserted hallway. "I'm placing you with Mrs. Steadry. You're a bit behind, in Arithmetic, Reading and History but it's important to be with students the same age as you." He stopped and opened a door marked Seventh and Eighth Grade.

A small dark headed woman wearing a red dress smiled as they walked in.

"Hello, Mrs. Steadry," Mr. Shanks said. "I want to introduce Gladys Lee Simmons. She's been testing all day." He handed a file folder of papers to the teacher. "I'll leave you two ladies to get acquainted. Gladys, I had Miss Vaughn run by the Katy and tell your brother that you'd be late."

"Thank you," Gladys said.

"Now, have a seat and tell me about school in Leedey while I look through you scores." Mrs. Steadry sat down and pointed to an empty desk near her own.

Gladys smoothed her skirt and sat, "Pa wouldn't let me go much after my ma died and then I didn't want to go. I was almost through the fifth reader and I can figure some."

Gladys sat silently.

Her teacher placed her glasses on the desk and with a reassuring smile said, "I see you're thirteen years old. We have some work to do. Your scores show that you are at the beginning of sixth grade. By law, you must stay in school until you've completed the eighth grade and I hope you stay with us through high school."

"Does this mean I gotta go to the sixth grade class some?" Gladys anxiously picked at her fingernails. "I've always been the biggest in my grade."

"Mr. Shanks put you here, and here you'll stay. Come in a half hour before school starts and we'll work together at getting you caught up with your peers."

"I'd be glad to come in early and I don't mind working hard to catch up," Gladys said with a sigh of relief.

Mrs. Steadry smiled and retrieved a book from her desk. "Gladys, do you mind erasing the board for me? I see you have very nice penmanship, and it would help me a lot if you wrote these eighteen frequently misspelled words on the board. Tomorrow I will give the definitions for this weeks' spelling lesson."

"Yes, ma'am."

Hearing the words of praise she picked up the damp rag on the shelf of the chalkboard, erased it and then wrote:

1. coyote
2. extinct
3. decision
4. disease
5. embarrass
6. familiar
7. government
8. grammar
9. judgment

10. independent
11. occurred
12. pneumonia
13. privilege
14. separate
15. separate
16. vacuum
17. Wednesday
18. naturally

Very nice," Mrs. Steadry remarked when Gladys finished her last word. She put on her coat and helped Gladys with hers. "What a beautiful coat you have. I'll walk you home."

Gladys smiled and gathered up her book bag. Mrs. Steadry took her purse from her desk and they left the room.

"Ma'am?"

"Yes?" They walked through the darkened hallway and down the steps of the school.

"Would it be okay if I didn't read aloud until I'm caught up? I promise I'll read every night and try real hard."

"I think that'll be fine. We'll start practicing in the morning."

Mrs. Steadry talked about schoolwork as they walked. Gladys listened but her thought were elsewhere. She looked around at the lights shining in town. The store windows were dark, but the houses were pretty with lamps and lace curtains framing the picture windows. The farm was gloomy at night.

They stopped at the door of the Katy. Gladys bid her teacher goodnight and stepped inside. Bud was playing horsy with Lucille and Estelle was putting supper on the tablecloth. They used the last three places of the counter as their table and Lucille's highchair made the fourth seat. They all looked at her as she came in.

"You must have had quite the day," Estelle said and looked at the clock that read half past five.

"I did!" Gladys put her book bag on a stool and hung up her coat, then continued in the same breath. "I'm in the eighth grade, even though I should be in the sixth grade, I'm goin' in early for extra learnin' time with Mrs. Steadry, she thinks I have nice handwritin' and I got to write spellin' words on the board and I took tests all day and I need to use the privy." Gladys ran out the back door.

Bud and Estelle looked at each other.

"So much for a case of nerves," Bud laughed and sat Lucille in her high chair.

Estelle buttered a roll and gave it to her daughter. Lucille crammed it in her mouth, so she grabbed it back and tore it into pieces.

The back door slammed and Gladys washed her hands at the sink.

"Sis, start a little slower and tell us about your day." Bud put a piece of ham on her plate, Estelle spooned succotash and handed her a buttered roll.

Gladys took a huge gulp of milk and said, "I spent most of the day in this little ol' supply closet . . .

# CHAPTER FOURTEEN | LETTERS BETWEEN JACK & GLADYS

*1924 to 1925*

December 2, 1924

Dear Jack,

I like it here at Bud's fine. I know you don't remember him, except when he came to the funerals. He has a pretty wife and a baby named, Lucille. Bud's wife, Estelle says I got to go to school and then I can help cook after school and on Saturday. I like school. I always had trouble learning before, but now it comes easy. I read a lot of books. I like <u>Little Women</u> and <u>Little Men</u>. Both books are by Louisa May Alcott and she writes about her sisters. One of the sisters dies, just like us.

I wish you were here with me. Someday we will be together. Keep writing me letters and drawing pictures. I'm sending you a dollar for your birthday. Buy a few stamps but spend the rest on candy or something fun.

Love,

Gladys


January 10, 1925

Dear Gladys,

I did what you sade and bot stamps and candy and a nickel tablet. Teacher helped me write.

Love,

Jack


February 28, 1925

Dear Jack,

You write nice. I appreciate the picture you drew me for my birthday. I'm fourteen now and I had my first birthday party. We had cake, ice cream, and cherry cokes and played cards.

*I am now in the eighth grade and Estelle studies with me and I read to Lucille. I love history.*

*Arithmetic is still hard. I understand it in my head but getting down on paper is hard. I just finished a book called the <u>Five Little Peppers</u>. The Pa died and left the Ma to care for five children. They get to stay together and live in a rich house with their Ma and new Pa, the doctor that took care of Polly. I wish you were here.*

*Bud says you can live here now if you don't mind sleeping with me in the kitchen. They'll get you another rollaway.*

*Love,*
*Gladys*


*March 25, 1925*
*Dear Gladys,*

*I missed you so much last nite that when Pa came in to bed he was mad that I was crying. He red your letter and said I can't live with you.*

*Send my letters to my teacher from now on and she'll give them to me. She's helping me with this letter and makes sure I spell things right. I aim to come see you soon.*

*Love,*
*Jack*


*April 4, 1925*
*Miss Hull*
*Washington Grade School, Oklahoma City*
*Dear Miss Simmons,*

*I am Miss Sarah Hull. Jack is a sweet boy and misses you a lot. He is quite bright, but a bit behind. I will work with him after school. I teach the younger children and he will be in my class for a few years. I am happy to receive your letters and anything else you wish to send Jack.*

*Sincerely,*
*Miss Hull*

April 12, 1925

Dear Miss Hull and Jack,

I'm happy Jack has a friend and someone to help him. I won't worry so much. I've been reading books about people. They are called biographies. One was about Florence Nightingale. She was very brave and went out on battlefields to help soldiers who were hurt. The second book was about Jane Addams. She helped people who lived in Chicago and were poor.

Estelle says if I save my money from working there is no reason I couldn't go to nursing school. I'm thinking on that.

Bud says to write and tell us if you need clothes or school things. Tell me what books you are reading. Do you have many chores?

Love,

Gladys


April 21, 1925

Dear Gladys,

I help Miss Hull at school, cleaning chalkboards and other stuff. I'm airing tires and checking oil in a gas station on Saturday. I work for tips. I'm gonna buy me some clothes. I don't know what Pa and Daisy do all day. They are always cranky to me so I stay away. I ain't read nothing fun yet except what's in my books. I like listening you tell me stories instead of reading.

Love,

Jack


May 5, 1925

Dear Jack,

I know it's not your birthday, but here is three dollars from me and five from Bud and Estelle. Buy what you need for school. I want you to look nice for school and church. You mind me and if you need more, let me know.

Love,

Gladys

*May 17, 1925*

*Dear Gladys,*

*I grew out of my overalls and short pants. Miss Hull helped me pick out shoes, trousers and a couple of shirts. I got a union suit for next school year and other stuff. I got a lunch bucket and a strap for my books and pencils and paper. I had some money left so I treated both of us to an ice cream. I didn't think you would mind. She got strawberry and I got chocolate. I love chocolate ice cream. Miss Hull gave me a jacket that belonged to her little brother that died. I don't need it now, but I will in the fall.*

*I asked Miss Hull to marry me. She's thinking about it.*

*Love,*

*Jack*

*P.S. I sleep with Pa and he snores. Daisy is a good cook, but not as good as you. Jake her biggest boy, goes to school with me. She packs a good lunch that we share. We get a biscuit or corn bread smeared with jam and butter and a slice of ham and a sweet or apple if she has any. I make him carry the pail, 'cause I'm bigger.*

# Chapter Fifteen | School Days

*April 1925*

"Please Bud take it down. It's so embarrassin' having my report card up on the wall."

"You made up a powerful amount of work in five months, and I'm proud of you."

I couldn't have done it if Estelle hadn't helped me with my sums and multiplication tables and Mrs. Steadry with my reading. She said I'm a fast learner."

"I can't help tellin' everybody how smart you are."

"I appreciate it, but I ain't the only one who got good grades."

"True," Bud said and he handed the offending document to her.

She took the paper from him and put it in her history book. "I never liked learnin' before."

"Do you want this shake straight or with malt?"

"Straight, please. I'll sit here and study. We have a big test Friday on the constitution and we gotta pass it to get outta eighth grade. Where's Estelle?"

"Estelle and Lucille went to the bank with the deposit," Bud poured the shake into two glasses. "How you fixed for pocket change?"

"Estelle gave me a dollar and is depositin' the rest," Gladys put two straws in her glass and sucked noisily. "I can't get anythin'."

"Here use a spoon," Bud said stirring his shake and gulping down a blob of ice cream. He slammed his glass down, "Gosh, my head is frozen."

He rubbed his forehead with his hand and sucked air between his teeth.

"Yeah and you're wearing the rest of it," Gladys said laughing and pointing at the ice cream on his apron. "Next time, I'll make the shakes."

"Jack sure appreciated the few dollars we sent. It's nice to know I can help him when I can."

"I'm glad," Bud said and washed the front of his apron with a dishrag from the sink.

Gladys took another slurp. "There, got somethin' that time. This is good, even if you do make a mess."

"You're funny."

"No I ain't, but I know a joke. What did the mayonnaise say to the icebox?"

"I dunno. What?"

"Close the door, I'm dressin'." Gladys laughed and took another big sip, which promptly came back through her nose.

"Now look who's making a mess," Bud chuckled and handed her a clean dish towel. He wiped the counter with a wet cloth that they kept in bleach water. "Good thing your aim was off and missed your history book."

"Teacher wants me to make a speech at Recitation Night," Gladys said. "She said I'm the most determined student she ever met and wants me to talk on the subject."

"That's quite an honor, Bit. Are you gonna do it?"

"I think so. I'll speak on the importance of bein' stubborn."

Bud smiled, "Stubbornness or determination is two sides of the same coin. Determination sounds better."

Gladys looked thoughtfully at him. "Maybe that's what I'll talk about. I like the way you said that."

She opened her black composition book and started writing. No one came in and they spent a quiet half hour. Bud dried glasses. He held them up to the fading afternoon light to make sure all the spots were gone before he put them away on the open shelves under the counter.

She asked Bud, "Do you think I would be less stubborn if Ma hadn't died? Does bad stuff change us and the way we are?"

He took the chair next to her and said, "Bit, you ain't stubborn, you want stuff explained and you want to be respected. Your determination is what's gotten you through."

Gladys said thoughtfully, "Bud, did you know Pa hates the way I look. He'd yell at me and Ma to do something about my hair. He said only an animal looks like I do."

"Have you noticed Lucille favors you and him.Do you ever thinks she's ugly?"

Surprised Gladys said, "Of course not. She's beautiful."

"And so are you." Bud rubbed an imaginary smudge on the counter.

Gladys chewed the end of her pencil and continued.

"I overheard him tell Ma, but she was already dead. Pa's folks were from Alabama. He ran away the day his brother died." Gladys spoke in a rush. "They had different ma's and was raised together because his brother's ma died, then he got gored by a pig and died of blood poison. Pa's a bastard for reals."

Surprised, Bud said, "He never talked that much to me in my life."

Gladys wiped her eyes with a corner of her cloth napkin. "He talked to her, not me. He never talked to me or even saw me unless 'twas a chore or something he don't like. Must be where I get it."

"Get what?"

"Talkin' to dead folk. I talk to Ma all the time, especially when I pray. Do you talk to Ma or other folk who've passed?"

"Can't say I do."

"You probably don't have to. You can talk to Estelle anytime."

Bud swiveled her chair, so they faced each other and somberly continued. "You're gonna be a beautiful woman. Everybody goes through a time of being awkward as they grow up."

"Okay, I understand." Gladys changed the subject, "Don't you think Lucille is funny and smart?"

"I know what you mean. It always surprises me to hear all those words come out of that baby's mouth. She talked and sang before she walked and hasn't stopped since she discovered words."

"She's a mess," Gladys replied. "I love that she snuggles in bed with me in the morning. She's so warm and loves to twist my hair in ringlets."

"Sounds like her. I'm glad you two girls enjoy each other. Now, read me what you've written."

"Okay, but it needs polishin'."

*"Determination is necessary to succeed in life. If one does not have gumption or determination, when something bad happens one gets blown away like the foolish man in the Bible who built his house upon the sand. The winds came and blew his house down. His neighbor, the wise man built his house upon a strong rock and a firm foundation. That house withstood the storm. If one is determined or stubborn enough to stand firm when the storms of life hit, that person won't break. It is always a good thing to explain things to a determined or stubborn person so they can make up their own mind. My brother, Bud, told me this about me and I think he is right. I like to be given reasons for things."*

"That's all I got Bud."

Bud clapped and was joined by Mrs. Steadry who had arrived with Estelle and Lucille for a cup of tea. Lucille lay sleeping in her carriage.

The teacher sat down by Gladys.

"You wrote a wonderful essay, my dear. Now, take out the personal part about you and Bud and write a closing sentence or two and I would give it an A. Have you ever written a theme before?"

"No ma'am. This is my first," Gladys said and handed her paper to her teacher.

Lucille popped up and said, "Gwadys, wearn me wetters, so I write 'freme."

Gladys laughed at her two-year-old niece and said, "Let's wait until summer to work on that."

"My goodness gracious, genius must run in the family." Astonished, Mrs. Steadry said, "How old is that child?"

"Lucille started talking in complete sentences when she was fifteen months old." Estelle said and handed her a cup of tea. "She's talked nonstop ever since. We're used to it, but she does surprise folks. She turns three next January."

Lucille held up three fingers and snuggled in to resume her napping.

Bud smiled and put his one hand on Lucille's head and gave Gladys's shoulder a squeeze, "I'm mighty proud of my smart and pretty girls." He gave Estelle a wink.

"You have every right to be," Mrs. Steadry handed the empty tea cup to Estelle.

"That's the truth," Estelle said.

"Dat's da truff," Lucille mimicked, not sleepy at all.

"Remarkable and good-night," Mrs. Steadry said and left as the streetlights came on.

Later on that night, Gladys had never felt more peaceful as she settled herself in bed and said her prayers. "Thank you Mama and Jesus for Bud and Estelle and Lucille and please let Jack come and live here soon."

# CHAPTER SIXTEEN | CHANGE

*Summer 1925*

"Number two scrambled, bacon crisp, extra gravy."

"Cowboy with fries, double cheese."

"Egg salad on toast, through the garden, side of cottage."

"Biscuits and gravy, over easy, sausage."

Gladys repeated the orders back to Estelle and cracked eggs, slapped meat on the grill, popped bread in the toaster, scooped cottage cheese, and garnished the four plates with lettuce and a slice of tomato. The café was packed and Bud took orders from the customers in line. The train crew ate first, along with any passengers who managed to get a seat at the 17 stool counter. As soon as someone finished eating, the seat was filled by a waiting customer.

Estelle took orders, served drinks, and cleared the counter. Bud greeted everybody as they walked in. The trains ran through at least four times a day and in between times the regulars would drop in for a bite. Bud usually sat a bit and visited, but Estelle and Gladys kept busy refilling shakers before the next rush.

Sometimes, Estelle fussed at Bud to help, and he'd grab a dish towel and polish silverware to please her. Lucille talked a blue streak to anyone who would listen to her, so a neighbor woman watched her when the café got busy. After work, Bud made cherry sodas and they sat on the red stools and played with Lucille and talked.

Gladys took a moment and looked around. She realized she was happy. The Katy Coffee Shop's plate glass window sparkled in the sun. The café was a cheery place so unlike the dismal home she had shared with Pa and Jack. She adored Estelle. Estelle might fuss now and again at Bud, but never Gladys. Besides cooking for folks, Gladys bleached the shelves and liners every Monday afternoon and cleaned the icebox. There was always something to do and because she was a hard worker, she in turn had endeared herself to Estelle.

"Bud," Estelle said after the lunch rush was over and clean-up finished. "Gladys and me aim to run over to the Rexall to look at the new magazines and pick up a few things. You don't mind do you?"

"You go ahead, Kid. I think Lucille and me will do fine."

They looked at Lucille who was running the length of the room and twirling on the stools.

"If I need you, I'll just stand outside and holler."

They shared a quick kiss and then Gladys and Estelle put on their hats and stepped across the dusty street. Cars were parked and a few wagons and horses were tied up in front of the green grocers. A crowd was going into the Farrell's Dry Goods and General Merchandise.

"He has a new Philco," Estelle said. "He must be showing everybody how it works."

At the far end of town they could see the construction of the new hotel going up. The girls waved to the Church of Christ preacher as he watered the lone rose bush in front of the church.

"If he spent as much time visiting sinners and praying with the sick as he does on that bush, more people might get saved. This town hasn't had a baptism in over a year and the devil's always busy in the hearts and minds of folks," Estelle said emphatically.

They walked into the drugstore and saw Mr. Henry, the druggist, compounding in the back. The cosmetics and magazines lined the right side of the store. Cough and first aid remedies crowded the aisles. Tobacco and candy were near the door and register.

"Gladys," Estelle said, "let's take a quick peek at the magazines to look at the latest fashions; then I want new make-up for me and you. You're starting high school in a couple of weeks. I'm dying to take my tweezers to your eyebrows."

"You mean it? You're gonna teach me?"

"Gladys there's nothing to putting on cosmetics. Your complexion is nice. Why some girls have to fight blemishes with a bar of Palmolive, but you and I don't."

Estelle leafed through McCall's and Vanity Fair and Gladys looked over her shoulder and then decided to walk around the store. She eyed the Hershey bars, but decided chocolate might hurt her complexion.

Mr. Jones, the clerk, was stocking tobacco. He waved her over and shoved a can of tinned tobacco under her nose and said, "Have you heard the one about Prince Albert?"

"No, Mr. Jones," Gladys whispered and wished Estelle would come over.

"He's in the can and want's out. You better open it, girl."

Mr. Jones collapsed with laughter. Gladys thrust the can of tobacco away and hurried over to the cosmetics counter. Estelle joined her and expertly matched powder and lipstick to Gladys' complexion. She then added two Hershey bars and a tin of snuff for Bud. Gladys glanced nervously at Mr. Jones as Estelle paid for the purchases, but he did not speak to her again.

As they walked down the street, Estelle said, "I haven't heard the train whistle and I don't hear Bud hollering, so let's make some beauty appointments. Wauneta is a wonder with hair and has a new permanent wave machine. But we'll let her decide what to do with the both of us. Won't Bud be surprised!"

Gladys reached over and hugged Estelle. She had always felt ugly.

"Why, Honey," said Estelle, "you alright?"

"I'm just happy."

"Gladys, you saved my life when you came to work at The Katy. I'd been run ragged trying to keep up with everything and Lucille."

Estelle gave Gladys a squeeze in return and together they and walked into the Beauty Shop. The smell of ammonia about knocked her over. Pictures of models sporting the latest short bobbed styles were framed on the walls. Wauneta's had two chairs for styling as well as a small sitting area. The back wall was lined with two hair dryers and a machine with a bonnet and electric wires with curlers attached to them. Gladys felt weak in the knees just looking at that contraption.

Estelle inquired about appointments

"It just so happens I have an openin' right now," Wauneta said.

"Gladys, I want you to take that appointment. We're not expecting the rush for a couple more hours and Bud and I'll hustle if we get busy. "

"Estelle, really?"

"Really. I'll settle later, Wauneta. Bye" Estelle left quickly and hurried down the street.

Wauneta motioned for Gladys to have a seat. She unbraided her hair, took a rattail comb and lifted and scrutinized different sections of her hair.

"Hmm. Fine and curly and my guess is you want it straightened and cut."

"Yes ma'am. Whatever you think will look nice."

"The catch is you can't touch your head for three weeks. No combs, fingers, nothin'. The oil and dirt form protection on your scalp, so you don't get a burn from the chemicals."

Gladys made a face and said, "How do I keep neat, if I can't touch it?"

"If I did your hair today, it would fall out. That's why we gotta," Wauneta continued. "I'll put short braids in your hair and you'll wear a kerchief around it. When it gets messy, come see me and I'll put them in again. Remember, don't touch your scalp."

Gladys thought back to the day three years ago when her family had their portrait taken and how she had always felt like the maid or servant in her family. She thought about Pa being ashamed of her. She felt herself go hot with remembrance and shame. Mama always called her hair "a matted mess" and sighed whenever she tried to comb it. Daisy and Ivy had made fun of her, and never helped her fix up for church or special occasions.

She scrutinized herself closely in the mirror. If her looks on the outside improved, maybe how she felt on the inside would change, too. Deep down she did not think that make-up or new hair treatments would help. But she was willing to try anything. Besides, Bud, Estelle and even baby Lucille loved her. She had a home, job and a nice complexion.

"I'll remember." She sat back down, adjusted her skirt and Wauneta began to brush her hair.

# CHAPTER SEVENTEEN | THE PRICE OF BEAUTY

Anytime Gladys got close to Lucille, she pinched her nose and took off running. Estelle mumbled something about beauty having a cost and Bud just laughed. Gladys stayed close to the grill and refused to wait on customers. She was counting down the hours until her appointment.

Just her luck that they were in the middle of a heat spell and her head smelled like hamburger, sweat and itched so badly she sat on her hands to keep from scratching. But, today was the day she was going back to see Miss Waunetta.

After the morning rush she yelled "Bye," and ran to the beauty shop. She'd been back a couple of times for a redo of her braids, but today would be different.

Gladys reached the screen door of the shop, knocked and yelled, "Hey." Her normal reserve was forgotten in her excitement.

Wauneta came from her house that adjoined the back door of the shop.

"Well you look ready," Miss Wauneta said. "It's gonna be a hot one today."

"Cleo," she shouted.

A tall black woman entered with two glasses and a pitcher of lemonade. Gladys noticed that her hair was cut short and styled in a sleek cut. Cleo put the tray down and looked at her before leaving the room.

That was strange, Gladys thought.

"I'll explain every step," Wauneta said draping a plastic cape over her and turned on the overhead fan. Gladys felt grateful for the breeze. Wauneta took a thick tub of petroleum jelly and coated her hairline, neck and ears. "This is to protect you from the chemicals that would burn your skin."

She took a long roll of cotton and stuck it to the jelly and made sure the back of her ears and neck were covered. She poured lemonade and handed a glass to Gladys.

"I'm goin' to mix the chemicals together and then brush the mixture on a section of hair at a time. I make sure every strand of hair is coated with this relaxer. It smells awful and I have to wear rubber gloves. If any gets on your skin, be sure and wipe it off." She handed Gladys a wet rag.

Gladys sat there sweating and smelling under the cape. She sipped her lemonade and waited.

"Cleo!"

Cleo came in and Miss Wauneta appeared from behind the curtain where she had disappeared. She wore yellow rubber gloves and continued mixing something that smelled like rotten eggs making her eyes water.

"Open all the windows and bring in a couple of electric fans from the house."

"Yes Miss Wauneta," Cleo left the house door ajar. Gladys looked and saw a kitchen with yellow and white checked linoleum and gleaming chrome appliances.

Gladys could hear her banging and muttering to herself.

"Once I've applied all the relaxer, I'm gonna wrap your head in aluminum foil and then we wait for the relaxer to take the frizz out of your hair. It's gonna feel awful, but you gotta sit here and take it. Ready?"

"What about that contraption over there. When do I use that?" Gladys asked pointing to the machine with curlers dangling from it. "Estelle told me that would make my hair straight."

"She was wrong," Wauneta said. "Not for you. Ready?"

"Yes," Gladys said.

Wauneta worked quickly and did not get any solution on her skin. Gladys dabbed her eyes with the washcloth. Her scalp felt warm.

Cleo had come in with the fans, but Gladys had kept her eyes closed. She felt the cooler air on her face; she was steaming in the humidity under the cape.

"Now, take a drink and I'm gonna wrap you up," Wauneta said.

In no time, Gladys was sipping lemonade with an aluminum foil helmet on her head. Wauneta busied herself with cleaning things up and then sat down and sipped lemonade herself and looked through a magazine.

After ten minutes her head started to feel uncomfortably warm. Gladys fidgeted in her seat and Wauneta looked up and checked her hair.

"My head is getting hot, but I'm okay."

"That's normal."

After twelve minutes the top of her head felt like ants were biting her where she had snuck scratches. Her hand instinctively went up to scratch and Wauneta reminded her not to. She tried to distract herself and her thoughts turned to Jack. In his last letter he had gotten a used bicycle and was riding around OKC. He liked to watch the bulldozers and workers building the new road that would stretch from Chicago to California. The road would connect Elk City to Clinton and Oklahoma City.

"Miss Wauneta, I think my head is cracking open or on fire. Would you come take a look?" Gladys said. She squirmed and wanted to dump the lemonade of her head.

Miss Wauneta snapped on her rubber gloves and peeled back the tin foil until she found scalp and hair. "Your scalp is very red, but you're not on fire." She smashed the tin foil flat in place and said, "But let's go to the sink and wash this mess out."

Gladys leaned back and Miss Wauneta unwrapped the foil and turned the sprayer on her burning head. The cool water felt wonderful.

"I'm going to add the neutralizer now. This will stop the relaxer and keep your hair from falling out."

Gladys felt a cool liquid being massaged into her scalp and her head quit burning. After a few minutes, Wauneta rinsed and washed her hair with a fruity smelling shampoo. Gladys enjoyed the sweet smell compared to smelling like a hamburger or a chemical factory.

"Time for the conditioner and then cut, set and style. Feel your hair."

Gladys tentatively touched her hair. It was soft and silky smooth. Wauneta wrapped her hair in a towel and Gladys walked to the styling chair.

Wauneta towel dried her hair and began to gently comb it. For the first time that Gladys could remember it didn't hurt. She no longer remembered the pain of the process.

Wauneta sectioned her hair and clipped it into place. Taking a section at a time she trimmed and cut.

"Now watch closely. You're going to need to do this."

She pulled over a tray of curlers and applied green goo to each strand, wrapped it in crisp tissue paper and carefully rolled and secured each curler with a long bobby pin. She then twisted a long silk scarf around Gladys' head and then set her under a hair dryer on the lowest setting. Wauneta sat down next to her and talked loudly.

"You're goin' to have to sleep on curlers or pull your hair up in a high loose pony tail with a scarf around your head. Sleep with a pillow under your neck. You can buy shampoo, moisturizer and everythin' you need at the Rexall; I'll make you a list. Every ten days is often enough to wash your hair. Come to see me when your roots start getting curly. It won't take me as long or be near as painful."

"Okay Miss Wauneta. I understand."

Miss Wauneta patted her arm and said, "I'm gonna tidy up around here. I'll turn the fan on you and get more lemonade and make a list of everything you need."

Gladys took a little nap underneath the dryer. She woke with a start and was hungry, but she was anxious to see her hair.

Wauneta came into the salon, "Let's take a peek."

Going back to the styling chair for the last time, Wauneta took out the rollers and ran her fingers through her curls. Parting it on the side and flipping the ends under, she styled a shoulder length bob. She added a ribbon, sprayed on a pound of lacquer, and pronounced Gladys perfect.

"Now run along and tell Estelle she owes me eight dollars and here's the list."

"I'll take care of it," Gladys said. She handed Wauneta nine dollars and ran out the door. Her head felt so light. She wanted to sing and dance her way back to the Katy. All she needed was a touch of lipstick and some rouge.

If only her sisters could see her now.

# Chapter Eighteen | First Day of High School

*Fall 1925*

Gladys checked her satchel. Her gym blouse and skirt were freshly ironed and rolled up so they wouldn't wrinkle, and her new tennis shoes were in a paper bag. After checking her hair, she applied a coat of soft pink lipstick and slipped a cosmetics bag inside her satchel.

She opened the door from Bud and Estelle's bedroom and entered the café. Behind the counter, Bud washed dishes and Lucille stood on a step stool and dried. Estelle was at the grille frying up a mess of bacon before the train crew arrived. Mr. Sterling, a friend of Bud's, sat at the counter plowing his way through bacon, eggs and pancakes. He whistled when he saw her.

"Sterling, mind your matters before I get after you with this fry pan," Estelle snapped at him.

Putting her hands on her hips, Lucille stomped over in her red cowboy boots and scowled at him in an exact imitation of her mother and said, "Nuff Sterling."

"Alright Little Sis, whatever you say," Sterling laughed and choked on his coffee. Bud leaned over the counter to slap him on the back and Lucille kicked him in the shins with her boots.

Gladys put her satchel on a stool and snatched Lucille. "You can't be pickin' on the customers, Lucille. It's bad for business."

"I don't mind," Sterling said. "I get a big kick out of Lil Sis. I don't mean no harm by whistlin' at you. You look nice, that's all."

Estelle put a glass of milk, a plate of pancakes and bacon a few stools down from Sterling. Gladys picked up the food and moved to the seat next to him and ignored Estelle's hurumph of disapproval.

"What're you doin' today Mr. Sterling?" Gladys asked and poured warm molasses syrup on her breakfast.

"I'm takin' a load of supplies to the cattle camp north of Leedey," Sterling said. "I'll be gone a couple of days. It's about seventy miles round trip and I'm takin' my own team and wagon. Make more money that-a-way. Gotta git, don't wanna be late."

He winked at Gladys and Lucille and left forty cents under his plate.

Bud rang up 25 cents at the register and put the rest in the tip jar.

"Up Gwadys, I want up," Lucille tried to crawl up on the stool next to her. Gladys put Lucille on her lap and tucked dishtowels into both their collars. They swapped bites back and forth between them. It reminded Gladys of taking care of Jack when he was young.

Taking a last drink of milk, she got up and placed Lucille on the stool. "I gotta run. Want the rest of my milk?"

Lucille nodded her head up and down.

Gladys helped Lucille take a long gulp of milk and wiped both their mouths with a cloth napkin. Using the underside of her spoon as a mirror she reapplied her lipstick. Lucille puckered her lips and Gladys dabbed a bit.

In the distance a train whistle hooted, signaling the arrival of the eight o'clock train. The sound reminded Gladys it was time to leave for school.

"I wish I could be two places at once and help you and Bud today," Gladys said to Estelle as she gathered up her things.

"Don't worry 'bout us," Estelle said and whisked eggs in a bowl. "Study hard and have a good time. We both left school early and we want you and Lucille to graduate."

"Me, too and I'll be home right after school."

"Gwadys, bring me candy," Lucille said."

"There's no candy in school, it's at the store," Estelle said as she scrambled eggs. "I declare, Lucille, you're something else these days."

"Hershey bar, and I gotta go," Lucille said, hopping up and down.

Gladys chuckled, grabbed her satchel from the counter and her lunch from the icebox and left.

"Well come on then. Bud, mind the eggs," Estelle said and took her daughter's hand and walked into the bedroom. She knew the train crew would tromp through the door at any time mingling the smell of sweat and coal with the aroma of bacon and coffee.

"Hot coffee comin' up boys, with bacon and eggs," Bud said a few minutes later as he served the crew. "Estelle will fry you up some pancakes as soon as she's done tendin' Lucille."

"Sounds great," the engineer said. "Saw that sis of yours sashayin' down the street. Where's she off to today, lookin' like a movie star?"

"School. And Gladys don't sashay. Remember she's only fourteen years old," Estelle glared as she came back into the diner with Lucille. "Go play Lucille while I finish up these pancakes and then we'll go to market and get some more eggs."

"And a candy bar," Lucille knelt on a quilt and fed her doll with a bottle of disappearing milk.

Estelle flipped pancakes onto plates and slammed them down in front of the hungry men. "I'll be back in a minute, Bud," and went to the corner and took Lucille's hand. "Bring Susie." They hurried out the door.

"Why's her dander up?"

"Gladys is attractin' some attention," Bud said.

"Should've left her a Plain Jane then," the crewman replied.

The trainmen slurped and chewed noisily. Bud kept the coffee and pancakes coming. He knew from experience the crew had to get back to the train and had just a few minutes to eat.

"Put breakfast on the railroad's tab. We'll settle up next time," the engineer said as they got up to leave.

"No problem," Bud waved at them before clearing plates and putting them in the hot soapy dishwater. He got a rag and wiped down the counter and reset for the next customers. The eight o'clock train was freight and didn't carry passengers like some of the other trains. He expected the local coffee and pie crowd at any time. He cut peach and chocolate pies and put fresh coffee in a pot and listened to it perk. He looked up and Lucille was trying to open the door for her mama.

"Hello girls. Lucille, where's my mornin' sugar?" He asked and opened the door.

He picked up his little girl and hugged her tight. Lucille found his face and putting her chubby hands on it she planted a kiss on his cheek. Wiggling to get down, she pulled a Hershey bar from her overalls' pocket and handed it over.

"Mama says share with Gwadys." Walking over to the corner she frowned, plopped down and stuck the bottle in Susie's mouth. "Susie's hungry and don't like 'terrupted to get eggs."

Estelle finished storing the eggs in the icebox. Smiling, she put her arms around her husband and kissed him on the mouth. "There's some sugar from me and I'm not cranky, anymore."

"You okay, Kid?" Bud asked, returning the kiss and looking into her green eyes.

"I am, but I aim to have a talk with Gladys. She's turned into a beautiful swan, and I don't think she's ready for the attention."

"We'll keep an eye on her, but like she said to Lucille, you can't be rude to the customers."

"I know and I'll give her some advice on how to handle herself. I met you at her age."

"Yep, and you certainly tried to scare me away. Any regrets?"

"No, but I wish I could've graduated. I want our girls to get as much schooling as they can."

"I want both of our girls to be happy in whatever they do," Bud replied, still holding her tight.

They heard a soft snore. Lucille lay curled up on the quilt sound asleep and hugging Susie.

"We're gonna have our hands full with that one," Bud said. "Maybe you can go back to school some day and get your diploma."

Estelle looked at him and said, "I would like that, but time will tell.

"It usually does," Bud said. "Coffee before the crowd gets here?"

"Sure and let's split a piece of that peach pie. I added more nutmeg than usual and I want to be sure it isn't ruined."

"Your pies always taste good, but I wouldn't mind a bite or two," Bud said as he dished up a piece of pie and handed a fork to Estelle.

Looking at her husband, Estelle pierced the crust with her fork and fed the first bite to her husband.

Smiling, he chewed slowly and said, "Perfect and I ain't talkin' about the pie."

# Chapter Nineteen | Fifteenth Birthday

*February 1926*

*February 24, 1926*
*Dear Diary,*
　　*Today's my fifteenth birthday. Bud and Estelle gave me this diary as one of my presents. I'm writing everything down because I don't ever want today to end. Nobody can read it unless I let them and it's a relief to have a place to write down my feelings. I'm wearing the key around my neck.*
　　*Bye, more later.*
　　*I aim to tell you everything that happened today. My favorite thing? Estelle and Bud gave me a party with a DECO-RATED BIRTHDAY CAKE! Estelle made it and wrote, "Happy 15th Birthday, Gladys!"*
　　*They sure fooled me. Estelle told me to take Lucille on a walk. Bud joined us and he took us west of town. We didn't get back until the streetlights were coming on, but the diner was dark.*
　　*Bud told me to take Lucille inside while he checked the fuses.*
　　*He walked around to the back and Lucille and I went in. The lights went on and people yelled, "Surprise!"*
　　*Lucille jumped up and down and popped balloons. Estelle scolded her and hugged my neck. Bud fed nickels in the juke box and started pressing buttons for songs.*
　　*We all started dancing together and nobody paired up except Bud and Estelle and the Compton's from next door. All of them are good dancers. Mr. Sterling wanted me to dance with him, but Estelle said no.*
　　*I could have danced all night, but Estelle reminded me it was time to open presents. My friend Patsy gave me stationery and I got the prettiest embroidered hanky from Mrs. Compton. Bud and Estelle gave me a little cedar hope chest that locks. My name is written on it in mother of pearl. Estelle said she would help me piece a quilt top to fill it. Bud invited Mr. Sterling to the party and he gave me some daisies in a mason jar. Estelle didn't like it much, because he's older than me, but I think he's nice.*

Bud lit the candles on the cake and told me to make a wish, but don't say what it is or it won't come true. He sure knows a lot about birthdays. I hated cutting that pretty cake with yellow roses all over it. Everybody ate big pieces and there's half a cake left. It was chocolate on the inside, my favorite.

We danced some more. Bud and Lucille danced, and she stood on his boots while he whirled her around the room.


February 25, 1926
Dear Diary,

I finally went to sleep, last night around two. I slept in this morning and missed Sunday school. I barely made it to worship service on time. I asked Estelle why she didn't get me up. She said you only turn fifteen once in your life and if Lucille hadn't gotten them up, they would've slept in, too.

Brother Pierson preached on the evils of dancing and how it puts impure thoughts in your head. I started feeling guilty for dancing last night. But then I decided dancing is like joy and Saint Paul tells us to be joyful, so I'll just put Brother Pierson out of my head. Never thought I'd be happy after Ma died, but here I am. I only wish I could see Jack. When I think about Pa, I feel like I've done something wrong. That ain't good.

Sometimes I think about what I overheard and how Pa treated me because I remind him of his ma. That don't make sense to me. I love it that Jack looks like Ma. Why wouldn't you want someone around that reminds you of someone you loved?

I like the song, Sweet Hour of Prayer. Bud has such a beautiful voice. He sings tenor and Estelle sings off key. Sometimes I don't hear the shape notes the way they are written in the hymnbook, and I sing a mix between tenor and alto- something strange. But I like singing and so does Lucille. She's only three but she sings the melody loud and clear. She's a stinker. If I sit by her in church, she teases me by tickling my hand or whispering and Estelle shoots us looks to behave.

She's always saying or doing something funny.

Mr. Sterling usually sits in back of us. Bud and him stick their legs out in the aisle because there ain't enough room in the pew.

After church we ate leftover cake and Bud made hamburgers. Then we all took naps. Lucille woke me up around four and wanted to go on a walk. Bud and Estelle were worn out from the party and still tired. Anyway, we walked downtown and window-shopped. Anthony's had little girl outfits displayed in their picture window.

Lucille stopped walking and just stared and pointed at the window at the cutest sailor hat she'd ever seen. She wondered if Estelle would buy her the hat.

She started swaying and imitating Brother Johns, our song leader at church, by humming and singing, Let the lower lights be burning, send a gleam across the waves, some poor, drowning, drunken, seaman, you may rescue, you may save.

I bent down and asked her what the words meant.

"I dunno, 'bout a sailor hurt?"

She was so solemn and sincere that I told her I would get her that little sailor suit and hat by putting it on lay-a-way come Monday.

She wanted to know what that meant. I told her it was when you put money down on something you want and then come in once a week to the store and make payments until it's paid for. I told her she could have it in about a month.

She hugged my waist and took off skipping down the sidewalk and skipped smack dab into Mr. Sterling. She pulled him right over to Anthony's and made him look at that outfit. She started jabbering about layaway. I about died. That child don't ever know when to hush her face. He got all tickled when she started singing that hymn again. He grabbed her hand and she grabbed mine and we swung her on down the street all the way to the Katy. Bud and Estelle were sitting out front eating ice cream sodas. We sat down on the steps and ate some. Mr. Sterling ate too.

Mr. Sterling chews tobacco and spits. Estelle told him he had to quit because Lucille chews gum and spits wherever she wants.

We watched the stars come out. Bud fetched his guitar he keeps in the bedroom hanging above the treadle machine. He and Sterling sang soft and low the way they sang to the cattle. Lucille went to sleep against me and I nodded off, too. She jerked and we both fell off the step and that was the end of the concert.

# CHAPTER TWENTY | A WALK IN THE COUNTRY

*Spring 1926*

Gladys often walked the red dirt roads outside of the Café when the town and people started closing in. It gave her time to think and be by herself. She felt grateful to Bud and Estelle, but sometimes she missed the open spaces of the farms and the hidey hole she and Jack had made in the barn away from Pa. Mostly she missed Jack and wondered if he was okay.

It was four months past her birthday, but today she felt old. She missed Ma. Sometimes she felt so numb she wanted to stab herself with a hat pin just to feel something. She didn't bite her fingernails or pick at her head anymore, but that didn't mean she felt better about the past. It was shut away someplace in her soul's hidey-hole.

Two and a half years since sickness took Ma from her.

She felt confused. Patsy Jane, her best friend from school, had just married Mr. Madison, an old widower with three kids. How could Patsy leave school and go be somebody's ma?

She thought back to her conversation with Patsy a couple of weeks ago.

Over sodas Patsy confidentially said, "His children need a mama and he proved up his land a long time ago. Ma says he's established and Pa says I can't do no better."

Gladys whispered furiously back, "Farmin' and takin' care of kids is a lot of work. Pa and me and Jack worked our farm after my Ma died and 'bout wore out. It was awful." Gladys shuddered in remembrance.

"Don't be such a wet blanket," Patsy said quietly narrowing her eyes and tossing her braids. "You were just a little girl. Besides, Bertha'll help me. I want you to stand up with me at the Preacher's. We're gettin' married just as soon as Ma finishes my new dress."

"You gotta be kiddin' me," Gladys said, no longer bothering to whisper. "What do you know about cookin', sewin', tendin' chickens and hogs, cannin' and cleanin'? And don't forget havin' babies. Bertha won't be helpin' except when school's turned out."

Patsy turned on her and shouted, "I expected you of all people to understand, bein' next to an orphan and livin' on the charity of your brother. If you can't be happy for me, don't bother comin' to the Preacher's to see us married."

The Café was empty, but hearing her yell, Estelle came in from the bedroom and saw Patsy dashing out of the door, braids flying.

Gladys had her head down on the counter and in a muffled voice told Estelle what had happened. Raising her head she said, "I had to tell her the truth. She has no idea how much work there is to runnin' a farm. She's chasin' after a dream and a new dress."

Estelle rubbed her back. "I think you did right by her. You told the truth from your own experience. It's up to her, but I think she'll go ahead and get married. She's sixteen and the law says she only has to stay in school through eighth grade."

"Is it true what she said? Am I livin' on charity?"

"I've told you before Gladys, you aren't a burden. You eased our load considerably when you came to the Katy. Now put your things away and turn the sign to closed and lock the door. I've got soup on the stove and the rolls have risen. Let's get supper ready."

Estelle had eased her mind some, but something Patsy had said about being an orphan bothered her like a pebble in a shoe. She didn't want to be married and she certainly didn't want kids, but it would be nice to be special to someone.

If truth be told, she kinda liked Mr. Sterling, but he was more Bud's friend. She knew Estelle didn't like him much because Bud occasionally went drinking with him on a Saturday night. She considered Sterling a rough character.

"Sterling's a bad influence." Estelle would scold Bud, "I know he's your friend from rodeo days, but he's too rough to be around Gladys and Lucille."

Still, Gladys thought he was kind and liked that he treated her like a lady.

"I'll go wadin' in the creek," Gladys said to no one as she scrambled through the blue stem grasses to the soggy bottom of the hollow. She took off her shoes and socks and rolled up her overalls. The mossy water was cold and little minnows nibbled her toes. The cottonwoods provided a green canopy of shade. She sat down on a big rock in the middle of the shallow water and picked a blade of grass. She stretched it between her thumbs and blew a thin reedy sound, joining the afternoon song of the birds. Glancing at the water, she saw a rock glint in the sun. Reaching down she picked it up and saw it was an arrowhead. Bud had told her that the Cheyenne camped around by the creek bottoms before they got run off by the cavalry fifty or so years ago. General Custer had led a massacre of Indian women and children before he met his own end. Served him right, Gladys thought.

She tucked the arrowhead in her pocket and waded further along the stream bed. Water always made her feel better. The wind rustled strongly through the trees and bent the prairie grass. Clouds cast a shadow, but she didn't notice.

The Katy was never quiet and was too small for privacy. She got up early, after Bud left, and dressed in the bedroom with Estelle while Lucille slept in her little trundle bed. She always had to attend to women stuff in the privy and she and Estelle both agreed it would be nice to have an indoor toilet and bath tub. Whenever they wanted a bath, they had to drag the hip bath from the shed and heat the water on the stove.

She missed Jack and playing with him.

Pa was a lost cause to her. He wouldn't let Jack come and visit and he and Daisy never asked them up. Talking with Bud and Estelle about him had eased her heart some, but it didn't stop the feeling that she was really and truly an orphan.

Concentrating so hard on the past, she didn't notice the buildup of black clouds in the northwest. The sky grew darker and a gust of wind dumped her in the creek, and she dropped her shoes and socks.

"Well I never," she said and chased them. She looked up and saw the angry looking clouds and noticed the cottonwoods rustling overhead. She put on her dripping shoes and socks and began trotting towards town.

A low, fierce growling carried by the wind caught her attention. As she turned onto the red dirt road, she looked back to the northwest and saw a mass of green and black clouds boiling about a half mile away. A long, finger descended from the clouds and touched the ground.

I'm in for it now she thought and started running.

Sweat poured down her face in the hot humid air and she used her damp shirt to wipe her eyes.

"Ow," she exclaimed as something hard hit her head. She was being pelted by hail and knew she needed to get underground.

She put her arms over her head and ran as fast as she could. Her eyes were protected, but the hail hurt her. She kept going. The howling increased and through it she heard someone calling her name. Glancing back, she saw Mr. Sterling and Beauty right behind her.

"Get on!" He shouted, barely stopping he awkwardly helped her up onto the saddle behind him. She grabbed him around the waist and bent forward. His back was broad and wet and smelled of sweat. She felt a quivering deep inside her belly.

Beauty was in a full gallop now racing towards town. Looking back, Gladys saw a fat finger of dark cloud touch down and follow the creek right where she had been.

"Ride harder, Mr. Sterling, it's gonna catch us if you don't," she shouted in his ear.

Sterling slapped Beauty with the reins. The town was just ahead. Leaves and tree branches whirled around them. The cottonwoods screamed as they were torn up by their roots. Gladys hugged Sterling tighter and squeezed her eyes shut. Her heart pounded and her mouth was dry.

We're gonna die.

Sterling cut across the train yard and they were in front of the Katy. Jumping down he pulled her from the horse and she ran towards the storm cellar. He slapped Beauty's rump. The horse took off in the opposite direction to outrun the twister. Sterling followed Gladys. Bud had the cellar door open. Scrambling down the steps they joined Lucille and Estelle.

Bud slammed the door with a crash and latched it shut. Overhead they heard hail bouncing off the door of the cellar and the sound of a train.

"That's the twister," Bud said as the crashing shook the cellar and something large landed on top of the door. Dirt fell off in chunks from the ceiling and sides.

"Mama, Susie's scared," Lucille's voice wavered as she spoke from Estelle's red checked apron where her face was hidden.

"I'll hold you both tighter," Estelle said gathering up both the child and the doll.

Bud handed them a quilt. Sterling took the quilt and wrapped it around them, putting his arm around Gladys. Gladys snuggled close and relaxed against him, enjoying his man smell and the warmth and safety of his body. The quivering in her stomach was replaced by a warm glow.

The tornado missed Elk City. A big cottonwood tree landed on the cellar door. After the neighbors pulled it off, they were able to open it. Bud made cold sandwiches and fed the town as people cleaned up. Sterling supplied the coffee that he made from a campfire in the side yard.

Estelle washed Lucille while Gladys took a tepid bath in the bedroom, telling Estelle how Sterling saved her.

Estelle then tucked both of them into the bed she and Bud shared.

She closed the bedroom door and walked through the café and went out front. She grabbed a sandwich and Bud gave her his seat and brushed a stray hair back from her cheek.

"How're the girls?" he asked.

"Exhausted. Gladys says if it weren't for Sterling she would've been caught in the tornado."

Sterling came over carrying two cups of coffee. He handed one to Bud and another to Estelle.

Sitting on the steps he explained, "I was ridin' back from Checker's place and noticed the storm. It started hailin' and I saw someone runnin' from the creek tryin' to make it to town. It was Gladys. I snatched her up on Beauty and brung her as fast as I could."

"Mighty convenient," Estelle sniffed. "I hope you weren't hoping to meet her secretly."

"What do you take me for, Estelle?" Sterling shouted, astonished at her nerve. "You may not like me much, but she's a young girl and I would never see her without askin' Bud first."

"Maybe we ought to be thankin' him, instead of questionin' his intentions," Bud interjected, looking darkly at his wife.

"I know you have feelings for her, and she may not know it, but she has feelings for you, tornado or not. You two were certainly cozying up in the cellar."

"My God, Estelle," Bud shouted. "I would have cozied up to Sterling, too, if he had just saved me from a twister. He don't deserve your disrespect."

"I'm just making sure everything is respectable," Estelle said. "She told me tonight how you saved her and she lit up talking about the ride on Beauty."

"Really?" Sterling pretended to not be interested. "More coffee?"

"Please," she said holding out her cup. "But be careful."

# Chapter Twenty One | Saturday at the Café

*Summer, 1926*

Taking a new piece of chalk, Gladys bit her lip and in her best handwriting wrote:

Lunch 35¢

| *Main Dish* | *Dessert* |
| --- | --- |
| Ham steak | Cobbler |
| Chicken Fried Steak | Chocolate Cake |
| Beef and Vegetable Soup | |
| | Cornbread Served with all Meals |
| *Sides* (choose two) | Iced tea or Coffee |
| Rice and gravy | |
| Apple sauce | |
| Cabbage | |
| Pickled Beets | |

I'll be sure and put plenty back for us," Estelle said as Gladys finished. "Coffee? And I recommend four jars of apricots for the cobbler."

"Sure," Gladys responded.

Gladys worked on lunch desserts while Estelle fried a pile of hash browns and bacon for breakfast. At seven o'clock she unlocked the door to the café and the first of the regulars strolled in.

Estelle filled plates and kept the coffee hot as more customers joined the group already seated. Gladys kept busy clearing the counter. She looked up and saw Lucille in her night-gown come in with her thumb in her mouth and dragging Susie.

"Mama, where's Daddy," Lucille asked.

"He's helping the farmers set up for market. Gladys, can you take over breakfast while I set this child to rights?"

"Of course," she said and quickly washed her hands.

"Mornin' all." She noted that every seat was full and several coffee cups were empty. She started making the rounds with the coffee pot.

"Any pie left from yesterday?" a farmer asked.

"Nope, apricot cobbler will be ready at lunch," she replied.

"Don't seem right to not have any pie to finish off breakfast."

"Sorry," she shrugged.

No one lingered over their coffee cups and breakfast today. Gladys rang up 15 cents, the cost of breakfast, 17 times and put the extra 60 cents in the tip jar. She cleared the counter, wiped it down with bleach water, and opened apricots for the cobbler.

"Looky Gladys, we're twins!" Lucille shouted as she came into the diner from the back room. Lucille was dressed in a white shirt and overalls and she climbed on a stool to eat her breakfast.

"Yes we are."

"Let's sit down and have a bite," Estelle said to Gladys, buttering a biscuit, and sat down next to her daughter as they shared a plate of eggs.

"I will as soon as I finish this." Sprinkling sugar over the top crust, Gladys set the timer for 40 minutes and placed the cobbler in the oven. "I'll put the cake in after that's done," she said under her breath.

"Have you made the cake yet?" Estelle asked.

"Almost," Gladys said. "I just need to add the vinegar, water, and oil."

"Don't put it in now or your cake won't rise."

"I didn't know that," Gladys said. She put the bottle of vinegar down and crumbled a biscuit on a plate instead. Adding gravy she sat down.

"You girls look so comfortable in those overalls; I'm tempted to put on a pair myself," Estelle observed.

"Well listen to that," Gladys cocked her ear towards the radio over by the supply closet. "I think I hear music instead of weather reports and static." All three of them rose and stood in front of it.

"Sure 'nuff," Lucille said. "That song's from church, right Mama."

"Right, Sweetie. It's called, 'Will the Circle be Unbroken.'"

"We sang it at the funeral," Gladys remarked. "It's about seein' people again in heaven."

"Like a ghost?"

"Nope. A ghost is scary," Gladys explained. "Dead people from heaven aren't."

The bell rang over the door.

"We better hustle."

Gladys placed her dishes in the sink. "C'mon Lucille, you can help me."

The new arrivals called their orders back to Estelle. Lucille stirred while Gladys added oil, vinegar and water.

The café door opened with a jingle and a family of five entered. Bud and Sterling came in with some other men from town. Estelle made a fresh batch of eggs, added milk to the gravy as every seat was filled again. Gladys checked the cobbler and determined it was done. She put the cake in the oven and shut the door with her foot.

Lucille was busy wearing the chocolate from the spatula.

"Come on Lucille. Put the spatula in the dishwater and let me clean you up."
Remembering how much she hated being cleaned up by a dirty dish rag, Gladys took a fresh cloth to clean up her niece and then she started washing dishes. Lucille kept busy drying silverware and putting it away under the counter.

"Look at Lil Sis," Sterling nudged Bud. "Just three and already workin'. I'll have to leave an extry tip today. Gotta keep that girl in red cowboy boots."

"Cowgirl and wanna tip for a candy bar." Lucille corrected him and stomped over holding out her hand.

"That's not how we do that Lucille," Gladys said. "Come back here."

"No, tip," Lucille yelled.

Estelle telegraphed a look to Bud and snatching her up he handed her back over the counter to Estelle.

Estelle set her on the counter and looked straight at her. "Finish your chores and when the day is done you can have a tip from the jar just like me and Gladys."

Lucille scooted down and sat on the floor with a plop. She screamed and kicked her heels.

Bud picked her up and grabbed a wooden spoon from behind the counter.

"Lemme go, Daddy, lemme go," Lucille yelled and flailed against him.

Bud held her tight and said, "Gladys, mind the counter. Estelle, come on."

They went into the bedroom and closed the door.

Gladys stood wide eyed at the sink, trembling and pale. She thought back to the beatings she'd received. All she could think about was Pa whipping her around the kitchen the day the threshers came.

Sterling noticed her alarm and came around to her side of the counter.

Speaking softly, he said, "Sit down while I handle this crowd."

He refilled cups of coffee and scraped dirty dishes before dumping them in the dishwater. The diner had been quiet, but conversation started again. Gladys heard Lucille start to cry and then suddenly stop. Gladys got up and washed dishes. Sterling dunked the dishes in the rinse water and placed them in the strainer to dry.

He looked down into her somber brown eyes and asked, "You alright?"

"I guess. I've never seen Bud so serious before." Gladys said. "You think Lucille's okay?"

"Lil Sis?" Sterling said. "Sure. She needs to know who's boss. It's like gentlin' a colt. Gotta curb her will, but not her spirit."

"My Pa used to beat me," she whispered.

"Bud's told me he was harsh, but Bud would never hurt Lucille."

The door to the bedroom opened and Lucille came out, hiccupping. Bud and Estelle stood in the doorway.

She climbed on her little step stool and stood by the sink. She said to the crowd, "Sorry, for havin' a fit." She curtsied, stepped down and gracefully walked to her parents. Bud bent down and hugged her tight, but she wanted her mama. Estelle sat down at the end stool and cuddled her daughter, whispering softly to her.

Gladys's brown eyes filled with tears. Sterling looked tenderly at her and said, "Like gentlin' a colt."

"I understand. Thank you," Gladys said giving his hand a soapy squeeze.

Sterling went back to drying and said, "Anytime."

# Chapter Twenty-two | Revival

*July 31, 1926*

*Dear Diary,*

*The revival preachers say if we harbor unforgiveness in our hearts we're going to hell, no matter if we're baptized or not.*

*I guess I'm going.*

*Estelle wants me to be baptized the Church of Christ way for forgiveness of sins. Getting baptized wouldn't do me any good anyways, because I have this spirit of spite towards Pa. If I don't get baptized and got hit by a train or the end of life came, I'd be keeping the devil company through all time and eternity. Seems I'm destined for the Lake of Fire either way.*

*These Jesus revivals are crazy. The only thing all three preachers agree on is that sinners are all going to burn up and you gotta be dunked to be saved. They squabble about everything else.*

*According to the Church of Christ preacher, the way the Baptist and Holy Rollers baptize is wrong and are going to hell for it. True baptism that takes is for the forgiveness of sins and the water washes them all away.*

*The Baptists baptize as an act of obedience and the Holy Rollers baptize to speak in tongues and handle snakes. I think all this getting wet and not going swimming or wading is nuts.*

*If you get baptized as a baby like a Presbyterian or Methodist, it don't work. I haven't ever been baptized and so everyone is after me. Estelle and them all go to the Church of Christ so when I do get dunked I'll get baptized that way, but not until later.*

*The Church of Christ don't use a piano or fiddle because they make music in their hearts like the first Christians. Anybody using an instrument is in danger of hellfire. They sing, "When the Roll is Called up Yonder," without instruments. This is the true way of like precious faith*

*I'm feeling a little sick writing about hell so much.*

*I went to all three revivals just for fun and they mostly worked the same. Each revival ran for five nights with a potluck supper beforehand. Tables were set up under the cotton wood trees and fried chicken,* three bean salad, baked beans, cobblers and all kinds of food was set out. After a long boring prayer, we ate. Old people first, then married couples, young women, men, and children. There's always plenty of food, but the kids don't like to wait.

Some of the ladies bring ambrosia or fancy gelatin salad. You have to wonder about that because it's a melted mess by the time it gets eaten. What's really disgusting is how some of the old grandpas stir their gelatin salad into all the food on their plates and slurp it down. It looks like pig swill. But I don't judge because that's a sin.

Mr. Sterling likes to eat with us. Ever since our narrow escape with the tornado, Estelle is nicer to him. She says it's her Christian duty to be kind to him. He always wants to know what Estelle and I made and then he fills his plate. I like him and my tummy still gets tingly when I see him. We visited the other revivals together and Miss Vaughn went with us. Bud and Estelle don't go because they are Church of Christ members and going someplace else would be an occasion for the elders to come and visit.

Bud and Estelle had an argument because Estelle thinks Sterling is courting me. He's thirteen years older than me and Bud says I'm safer with him than anybody else. I'm not telling her about my tingly tummy. Estelle told me to kick any boy or man in his man parts if he tries to get fresh, but Sterling is a gentleman.

The Church of Christ rented the tent first. We found seats about halfway down and fanned ourselves with Guardian Funeral Home Fans. The service began when an old guy led prayer and then we sang lively for a while. I don't care what kind of Christian you are; the hymns are all the same.

Fanny J. Crosby wrote a lot of them. She was a blind lady who was asked once if she minded being blind. She said no, because the first face she would ever see would be that of her Lord and Savior. I could never be that good. She must be one holy lady to be so well represented in all the hymn books.

After singing it got boring with another long prayer and scripture. The preacher yelled at us about drinking, gossiping, lusting, and all kinds of depravity. Anybody doing anything bad is going to hell. It was pretty scary and interesting at the same time.

Finally, we sang and an invitation was extended to sinners and backsliders. Sterling and I are in the sinner category because of not being baptized. Sterling told me to never make eye contact with the preacher or you'll be down front and on your knees before you can say, "Holy Ghost." So I lift my eyes and sing to the top of the tent.

We sang forever. The Church of Christer's liked, "Almost Persuaded." The Baptist sang "Just as I Am." I found out that the Holy Rollers were partial to, "Oh Happy Day, when Jesus Warshed my Sins Away." And everyone sings warshed instead of wash. Again, if enough people didn't come forward to repent, we kept singing. By the second week I could feel my hair grow at the Baptist Revival waiting for the preacher to finish his prayer.

But nothing else was happening in town so I kept going.

Things started to move after the closing prayers at all three. Those getting baptized left to get ready. Those rededicating their lives to Christ got surrounded by their Brothers and Sisters in the Lord who promised to shore them up and pray.

Then everybody went back to their seats. We threw some money in a basket and after a final prayer, tromped down to the creek while singing, "Blest Be the Tie that Binds."

The almost saved lined the creek bank and one at a time go down in the water and came back up without sin. They looked the same to me but wore the most angelic smiles I've ever seen on dripping wet people.

After all the sinners for the night were washed clean, ice cold watermelons got hauled from the creek and split open. We spit seeds by lantern light. That was the best part of the night.

I believe the Church of Christ ladies put on the best potluck. The Baptist had the best music. Their piano player used to bang out tunes in a saloon in Tulsa before being saved. For pure entertainment value you can't beat the Holy Rollers. They got so excited over one sinner being saved they spoke in tongues and somersaulted down the aisles and fainted. They call it slayed in the spirit and have people who just stood around to catch the fainters.

But the one thing that the Holy Rollers did beat anything. They had a burlap bag that was wiggling and the preacher reached inside and pulls out a rattlesnake! The reason is the Apostle Paul said their type of

Christian could get bit by a viper and not die. That preacher twirled a big old rattler around his head and spoke in tongues at the same time. I ain't too crazy about that Apostle Paul or that Preacher either.

Mr. Sterling had warned Miss Vaughn and me that we might have to leave and said we were going to sit in back. We left when the preacher got a little too friendly with the snake. That one service was enough for me. I shook all the way home and when Bud saw how rattled I was, he fixed us chocolate sodas with three scoops of ice cream. Chocolate can fix anything and after I ate it I told them, "If Sterling hadn't been there I would have been a baptized Holy Roller. I was so scared I felt faint, and anybody would have thought I'd been slayed in the spirit,"

Bud, Miss Vaughn and Sterling thought that was funny. Estelle looked grim.

The Church of Christ may be boring, but they're safe. This Sunday maybe I'll go forward and be done with the whole mess.

Three revivals in three weeks is enough for anybody. Sorry my grammar is bad, but I want to get everything written before I forget it.

The Fair comes to town soon and that'll be a nice change. I hope they bring an elephant.

# Chapter Twenty-three | County Fair

*Fall, 1926*

"Ah-choo!" Bud sneezed

"Bless you," Lucille said up on his shoulders.

"Sure is dusty," Gladys remarked as the family walked by the side of the road. "Is it always this windy at Fair time?"

"Usually," Estelle replied through a thin scarf around her mouth.

Gladys' bare legs stung in the wind. A scarf was tied around her hair to keep it from standing on end. She'd been so busy with school and work that she hadn't made the time for her normal hair routine. She had twisted her hair and clipped it back and got a shock anytime she touched her head.

She leaned forward in the wind and shouted up to Lucille, "I hear music, let's check it out."

"I wanna go, Daddy. Lemme down." Bud let her go.

"Come on Gladys," Lucille grabbed her hand and pulled her along. "I wanna find a blue pony and ride all the way to France."

Bud held out his hand to Estelle. "Those two are a pair."

She took his hand. "I love seeing them both so happy."

"Think the blue pony with the green saddle is who you wanna ride to France?" Gladys chuckled as they walked around the carousel that quivered in the wind and continued to play calliope music. "I think the purple pony with the green saddle and yellow sash is the prettiest."

"To see the queen's underpants," Lucille shouted and scrambled up on the blue pony.

They slapped the reins and bounced up and down together, shouting over and over, "I see Paris, I see France, I see queenie's underpants."

"Lucille, where do you get these ideas? Don't bother taking up for her, Gladys," Estelle scolded as she and Bud strolled up. "You both better get off. The rides don't open until noon. Goodness sakes, that music is so loud you can hear it all over the place."

Lucille ignored her Mama, slapped her pony with the reins and continued riding to France. Gladys swallowed her smile and dismounted.

Bud retrieved his daughter and placed her on the ground. "You two ain't ridin' anywhere," Bud said. "We gotta go. Come back when the carousel opens and then ride to France, England or wherever."

"You're as bad as those two, but maybe today is a day just to have fun," Estelle opened her pocketbook and gave Lucille ten cents. She tried to hand a quarter to Gladys, but she shook her head no.

"I have money from my tips," Gladys said.

They left the carousel and started walking towards one of three big white tents that billowed in the wind. Gladys looked around at the midway. She would like to try some of the games, she'd never eaten cotton candy, and she wouldn't mind a drink of ice-cold lemonade.

The wind blew them in through the flap of the Domestic Arts tent.

"Domestic Arts is just a fancy way to say cooking and sewing," Estelle grumbled and unbuttoned her coat. The tent was crowded with folks getting out of the wind.

"I'm gonna go look at the livestock. I'd rather eat food than look at it," Bud said. "I'll meet you you all at the food tent."

Without waiting for a reply, he strode off.

"Well, that's just like a man," Estelle muttered and unbuttoned Lucille's coat. "What do you girls want to look at? I have a few minutes before my shift."
"You workin' today, Mama?" Lucille asked.

"Just doing my Christian duty. It's only for an hour, and we're making money to send children in Chicago to the Clean Air Camps. Poor kids go for a week to have fun and breathe in the clean mountain air."

"Maybe I should help," Gladys murmured as they walked by the food to be judged. "Don't the canned jams and jellies look pretty? Like stained glass."

"Yes they do and I need you to watch Lucille, if you don't mind," Estelle reminisced. "I won two blue ribbons for peach pie and preserves right before I had to go to bed with Lucille."

"Bed? Why'd you go to bed?" Lucille scrunched up her nose in concentration.

"So you'd be born right on time and not too early," Estelle said and mouthed to Gladys to change the subject.

Gladys nodded and tugged Lucille along, "Look at the gorgeous orange and blue pattern on that quilt."

"That's called the drunkard's path," Estelle said. "And you never give that pattern to a bride, because it's an ill wish."

"An ill wish?" Gladys asked.

"It may be pretty, but you're wishing the bride a life of hardship with a wandering husband," Estelle explained. Moving on she pointed, "Now here's a pretty quilt pattern. This flower basket quilt would be perfect for a new bride. This quilt was made from flour sack scraps leftover from a dress or panties. Maybe the quilter was taught by her mama or grandmother how to sew and piece the pattern onto muslin squares in the evening. I should be teaching Lucille how to put scraps together now."

"Would you teach me, too? We haven't had time to piece a top for my hope chest you gave me." Gladys reached out and touched the quilt. "I just don't think as a bride I'd want a quilt to remind me of all the underwear I ever wore."

"Good point," Estelle agreed. "I have a box with quilt patterns that you're welcome to look through. Bud brought home some that belonged to your mama and grandmother."

"I would love that," Gladys said softly.

"Mama?" Lucille asked and tugged her coat.

"Yes, Honey," Estelle put her hand on her daughter's hair and looked in her light brown eyes.

"Mama, look at that one," Lucille pointed to a pink, yellow and white quilt." Susie and I want that one.

"You've picked out Sunbonnet Sue," Estelle said. "I made one of those when I was younger. I loved going out in the shade of the yard and sewing together a quilt top in the summer. I made the nine-patch on your bed, Gladys, and the double-wedding ring on ours."

"When things quiet down this winter we'll look through that box of your ma's," Estelle sighed. "It's hard to find time to quilt these days."

"Mama quilted when Granma came to visit. They would go through the scrap bag and let me play with the leftovers they didn't want. Granma would make me kerchiefs for my hair and I thought I looked pretty. Daisy would laugh and say I looked peculiar."

"Daisy's one to talk" Estelle snorted and looked at the watch pinned to her dress. "I only met her once, but she certainly was full of herself. Anyway, every young woman needs a scrap bag and a sewing kit. We'll set you both to rights, but I got to go. Lucille, be good and mind your aunt."

"K," Lucille said.

Gladys walked on and called Lucille over to her. They looked at a quilt that was one big house with a yellow cloth square for a window.

"There's a note about this one. This quilt is from Alabama and belonged to C. Simmons. I wonder what it's doing here?"

"That lady has our last name," Lucille walked around the quilt.

"Wonder what this all means?" Gladys shivered as if someone just walked over her grave.

"I dunno," Lucille said. "I'm thirsty."

"Me, too, let's get some lemonade."

"It ain't so blowy anymore," Lucille said when they walked out of the tent, the hot sun shining on them.

They started down the midway looking at the booths. Gladys threw five baseballs and knocked down three steel milk bottles and won a miniature china cat. She gave it to Lucille.

"Try for a bigger prize, ladies?" The carnival man pointed to a china teapot. Gladys told Lucille to keep the cat but decided to win that teapot. She spent a dime for ten baseballs and knocked down eight milk bottles. The man carefully wrapped up her prize. Lucille petted and purred to her cat and Gladys thanked the man.

"Looky, Gladys, lemonade," Lucille pointed as a gust of wind hit them hard.

Gladys and Lucille walked over to the barrel with a sign that said, "Lemonade, five cents a dipper." They saw chunks of ice and lemon slices floating to the top. Lucille's mouth puckered up just thinking about the cold, tart, sweetness.

Gladys gave the lemonade man a quarter and said, "I would like two dippers, please."

"It's your turn," Lucille said and handed the dipper to Gladys. Gladys took her drink and handed it back to the lemonade man and walked away.

"Let's go ride the Ferris Wheel." Gladys said.

"And then the Merry-go-Round." Lucille was hopping up and down. "Looky there's Mr. Sterling.

Sterling caught up with them and asked, "What are you two doin'?"

"We're gonna ride the Ferris Wheel." Gladys told him. "Would you hold the prizes we won?"

"Sure. You ride. Beth Anne is supposed to meet me."

They passed by the fun house and Gladys glanced at the mirrors and shrieked. Her kerchief was missing, and her hair had come undone in the wind. Most of it was standing on end all over her head. She fumbled in her pocket for a hair tie.

"Why didn't you two tell me that I look like I plugged my finger in an electrical socket?"

"I hadn't noticed," Sterling replied.

"Really?" Gladys looked at him. "I always notice if my hair doesn't look nice." Gladys twisted her hair into a bun and fastened it close to her head except for the wispy hairs she couldn't capture.

"Here we are at the Wheel. Why don't you two give me your things and get in line."

"Sterling, Gladys, Lucille! Wait up." They turned and saw Miss Vaughn hurrying towards them. "I was hoping to see you all. I want to ride the Ferris wheel," she said. "Can you wait a minute. I'm about to die of thirst and thought I'd get some lemonade."

"You go get something to drink." Sterling said. "The girls are riding first and I'm guarding the prizes and then we'll ride."

Lucille was bouncing up and down. The next car was theirs and Gladys lifted her up and placed her in the seat.

"Now you hold onto me 'cause we're goin' up in the sky." Gladys clutched her as the car moved backward and higher, as two more people exited, and a man sat down. The Wheel lurched and stopped as the routine was repeated three more times. Finally, the cars were loaded with new riders, and they were off.

Lucille shook the car and shouted with glee and asked, "Do you think we'll see France?"

"No, but I bet we'll see the Katy," Gladys said.

They rode around twice and suddenly, there was an awful lurch and grinding sound; the ride abruptly stopped.

"Uh-ho," Gladys said and she and Lucille peered down as did the other riders.

They saw Sterling hand their prizes to Beth Anne, and he and the ride operator started tinkering with the engine and generator.

Gladys asked Lucille if she could see the train coming into town. Lucille chattered away and they played 'eye spy with my little eye.' Gladys looked down and saw that besides Sterling, several men were using an iron pole as a lever, attempting to put a belt back on a big pulley. She couldn't tell what else was happening.

Miss Vaughn waved to them and mouthed, don't worry.

"Gladys, when are we getting off? I wanna ride the Merry-go-Round." Lucille fidgeted and started kicking her legs to make the car start swinging.

"Lucille, honey, the big wheel is a little stuck and we have to sit very still and wait. Can you see the creek?"

Lucille pointed and chatted about the train coming their way; then the ride lurched and the stopped, lurched and stopped so the riders could disembark. Every rider was given free tickets for three more rides.

"Oh goody," Lucille said. "I wanna ride to France."

"Good idea," Gladys said. "Let's give Mr. Sterling and Miss Vaughn tickets to ride, too."


Later as they walked home in the twilight, Gladys told Bud and Estelle what happened.

"You got to hand it to Sterling," Estelle said. "He sure knows when to show up and save you from tornados, holy rollers, and Ferris Wheels. It seems he's bound and determined to be around."

Bud was carrying Lucille who was fast asleep with her hands around her daddy's neck. "      That's seems to be the case," he said.

"You think he likes me?" Gladys asked.

"Either that or he's your guardian angel," Estelle said. "What do you think?"

"I think I like havin' a guardian angel," Gladys smiled.

Bud guffawed. "That's good to hear."

"I want you to be sixteen before anyone takes you out on the town and that includes Sterling," Estelle said sternly.

They reached town and home never looked so good to Gladys.

"If it's all the same to you," Gladys said as she put her purse away, "I think I'll spend Saturday helpin' in the café. I've had enough Fair for this year."

"Estelle and I only took today off. We wanted to give you an extra day to enjoy yourself," Bud said.

"How 'bout I help with the Saturday rush and then I'll go to the movies with Lucille."

*October 3, 1926*
*Dear Diary,*

*We went to the Fair and the Ferris Wheel broke down. Mr. Sterling helped fix it. Estelle thinks Mr. Sterling is my guardian angel or he likes me because he seems to save me from disasters.*

*But I do like having him around. He makes my tummy do flip flops.*

*The Fair didn't have an elephant.*

*I'm going to the movies with Lucille tomorrow and watch a Tom Mix cowboy film. Bud and Mr. Sterling love cowboy movies, too. She only takes off her red boots to sleep. Bud and Mr. Sterling have set up a sawhorse and tied an old boney steer head to it. They're teaching her to lasso and practice whenever the café ain't busy. Estelle says they sound like wild Indians.*

*I like Mr. Sterling. Estelle said I have to be sixteen before he can court me. We'll see. Maybe. I don't know.*

# Chapter Twenty-four | Sterling

*Late Winter 1927*

"Bud, ever since Gladys turned sixteen we can't turn around without bumping into Sterling mooning about. It isn't proper," Estelle slammed shut a drawer and said, "She thinks he hung the stars. Talk to him."

"And tell him what? You sure sounded like it was okay for her to start seein' him after savin' her from the tornado and holy rollers. You said yourself he was her guardian angel." Bud slammed a drawer of his own. "Make up your mind woman, is he okay or not?"

Only a thin plank wall separated the girls from the bedroom where Bud and Estelle were carrying on. The café sparkled in the late afternoon Sunday twilight. The smell of bleach added to the look of cleanliness. Gladys was reading to Lucille on the bright patchwork quilt.

"What's a Swamp Angel?" Lucille asked.

'I think she's Freckles' wife," Gladys started thumbing through her worn copy of <u>Girl Of the Limberlost.</u>

"What about...?" Lucille started to ask.

"Hush Lucille and play with your doll for a while. I can't make out what your Mama and Pa are saying," Gladys said.

"He's too old for her," Estelle said angrily.

Bud guffawed, "He's thirteen years older than her. I'm ten years older than you."

Lucille looked up at her and said, "I wanna know if the Swamp Angel likes butterflies."

"Of course she does. Everybody likes butterflies." Gladys handed her the baby doll, Susie. "Here feed Susie." Gladys concentrated harder to hear the conversation.

"He's our friend and you know he would never do anythin' to hurt her," Bud said. "He told us as much the night of the tornado."

"He's moving too fast," Estelle replied. "Gladys is our responsibility. I had already worked in the laundry and knew about people before I met you. She's too trusting."

"Maybe you're right, maybe not," Bud said. "But why don't we do somethin' else besides argue?"

The girls heard soft murmurings.

"I betcha they're kissin'," Lucille said and made noises on the back of her hand. "Are you gonna kiss Mr. Sterling?"

"No, and if you breathe or say a word of this to him, I'll never buy you another Hershey bar." Gladys warned. "Look at me, Lucille, I mean it."

"You wanna pinky swear?" Lucille asked solemnly. "If I break a pinky swear, the boogie man will get me if I don't watch out. I can't ever sleep."

"Okay, pinky swear."

They hooked fingers and spat into their other hands and shook.

"C'mon, lets wash our hands and get supper on." Gladys said.

She helped Lucille up onto her stool and turned on the water. They dried their hands on the roller towel and spread the tablecloth over the counter. From the icebox Gladys handed Lucille cold chicken, potato salad and slaw to put on the table. She poured iced tea and Lucille set the table.

"Let's give your ma and daddy a few more minutes."

Lucille made more kissing and smacking noises before going back and feeding Susie dinner.

Gladys walked over to the mirror hanging over the dishwashing sinks and looked at her reflection. Since coming to Elk City, she had grown taller and curvier. Clothes from Sears's catalogue fit her well because of her height. Her favorite outfit was a long-waisted soft jersey dress and cloche hat that framed her face perfectly. The first Sunday she wore her outfit to church Estelle said she looked beautiful and Bud nodded in agreement. She was wearing the dress now, but not the hat. As a rule, they stayed dressed in their Sunday best to set the Lord's Day apart from every other day of the week.

Gladys grabbed Lucille and danced around the room. She had that funny feeling in her stomach again and her heart felt like it was skipping beats. Lucille threw her head back and laughed when Gladys twirled her around.

"Maybe Sterling will take me to the movies or church or we could have a picnic lunch some Sunday," Gladys said and fell onto a stool.

"Can I go on a picnic? Lucille leaned against her and said, "Dance with me some more. That was fun."

Gladys touched her face and said, "No, time to eat. Knock first, but go get your Daddy and Ma."

When Bud and Estelle entered the room, Gladys noticed Bud's shirttail was out and Estelle's hair was mussed. Bud and Estelle ate and didn't say much. Lucille shared a chicken leg with Susie. Gladys ate slowly absorbed in her thoughts.

Someone knocked on the door of the café.

"We're closed," Bud hollered. But he went to the door and opened it.

"Hey Sterling," he said, not surprised at all. "Come in and have a bite."

Lucille started making kissing noises again.

"I just came over to see if Gladys wants to go to the picture show."

Gladys glanced over at Sterling and smiled and whispered loudly to Lucille, "Stop that!"

Sterling smiled back. Estelle glared at Bud and Sterling and looked like she wanted to skin them alive.

"Is your sister going?" Estelle demanded.

"She's meetin' us there with a friend," Sterling replied.

"Well, I don't know," Bud raised his eyebrows and looked at his wife.

"I just want to walk her to the show and then back." Sterling said. "I'll have her home by 8:30."

"It's a school night," Estelle said. "And Gladys needs her rest."

"Estelle," Gladys said. "I wanna go. I'll be home early."

Sterling grinned.

"You had this whole thing set up, Bud." Estelle swung around on her stool and stomped over to the door where the two men were standing. Poking Bud in the chest, she said, "I swan, you and Sterling are nothing but a pair of skunks. I wash my hands of the whole mess of you. Gladys, do what you want."

Estelle grabbed Lucille and Susie and slammed the door of the bedroom behind her. They all heard Lucille's startled cry and her Mama shushing her.

"Don't worry Gladys, she'll calm down. You two run on and catch that show. I'll be waitin' up," Bud said.

"I'll take good care of her," Sterling said.

"I know you will. Have fun."

Gladys took off her apron. Her stomach was in knots and her heart racing. From the bedroom Estelle was jerking open dresser drawers and talking about what skunks men were. Lucille's frightened cries emboldened Bud to brave the bedroom and rescue her. He came right back out without his daughter. Something shattered against the door and Lucille cried louder. The unsettledness of the family confused Gladys. Anger always did. Maybe she shouldn't go, but she wanted to and besides she knew Estelle would forgive her.

Gladys put on her hat and coat and walked to the front door of the café where Bud and Sterling stood talking. Sterling held out his arm. They left the café and passed the picture window. She looked at their reflection. We look nice, she thought, and at that moment felt happier than she ever had. She smiled at Sterling as they walked down Main Street.

*March 3, 1927*
*Dear Diary,*
*Tonight I saw The Gaucho starring Douglas Fairbanks and Mary Pickford. Mr. Sterling took me. We shared popcorn and we each drank a coke. At night, grown-ups go to the movies. Are we a couple? Don't know.*
*I hope Estelle isn't too mad at me.*

# CHAPTER TWENTY-FIVE | RUMMY

*Summer 1927*

"Rummy! Mr. Sterling, you gotta pick up a card," Lucille said. "You could've played that three on Pa's book."

"I need that extry card anyway. I'll show you why when it's my turn and I lay down," Sterling said and arranged his hand.

"If you two are done, it's my turn to play," Bud said as he drew a card and discarded a five of spades.

Lucille drew a queen of diamonds and laid down two books and a run, playing all of her cards. "I'm out and I beat you both. Pay up."

"Again?" Sterling said. "Who's been teachin' you to play cards?"

"You have. Now pay up!" Lucille stuck out her hand and popped her gum.

"I'll pay for us both," Bud said as he handed her two sticks of peppermint gum. "Don't be telling your Ma we're playin' for valuables. You know how she hates gamblin'."

"I ain't tellin' Ma nothin' as long as you pay up each time," Lucille said and handed the cards to her dad to shuffle. "Wanna play for two books and two runs?"

"I'm plumb outta gum," Bud said standing up to stretch his legs. He shuffled the cards and handed them back to Lucille. "What 'bout you Sterling?"

"You both wiped me clean. I can't stand my ground with you two card sharks," Sterling stood up and stretched. "I could eat a piece of pie. Any left in the pie safe?"

"One way to find out, let's go check. You comin', Lucille?"

"Naw, I ain't hungry," she coughed as she wadded up both sticks of Wrigley's and stuffed them into an already full mouth.

Mumbling she said, "I'm gonna listen to <u>Little Orphan Annie</u> and color,"

"Suit yourself," Bud said.

"Hey, ladies. Got any pie left?" Sterling asked as he and Bud set down at the counter.

"Two pieces of coconut cream and Gladys just finished a chocolate sheet cake. Take your pick," Estelle said and placed two cups of coffee on the counter.

"How 'bout we finish the pie and save the cake for supper?" Bud said. "Is that bean soup I smell?"

"Suits me fine," Sterling said. "Lucille beat both of us. Why don't you two take a break and play a couple of hands with her?"

"You smell the beans and ham bone I put on for supper. Let me finish icing this cake and I'll play and drink some sweet tea," Gladys said. "Strange, we ain't been busy at all today. I wonder where all the people are?"

"They'll be here when they get hungry, no matter if it is windy," Estelle said with a wink. "Let's play for gum. If I know that child, she probably swindled these two out of a pack or two."

"How did you know we played for gum?" Bud asked.

"If her jaw isn't flapping with words, she's got a wad of gum as big as her head in her mouth." Estelle said as she took off her apron and went towards the bedroom. She hollered, "I figured you three must be up to something. Grab a couple of packs by the register Gladys, and we'll show her a thing or two."

Gladys grabbed the gum and touched Sterling's shoulder as she breezed by on her way to the bedroom where Estelle was dealing the cards at the rickety card table. Lucille set her cards on a wooden stand Sterling had made her because her hands were too small to hold all the cards she needed to play. Gladys handed a pack of gum to Estelle and kept the other one.

"Two books, that's eight cards you have to lay down not including the one you discard to win," Estelle instructed. "You buy cards because I'm only dealing six. Now, sit up Lucille, turn off that radio, and prepare to get beat."

"How did ya know Ma? Did Sterling or Daddy tell on me about the gum?"

"Nobody said a word, but I didn't fall off the vegetable truck yesterday," Estelle said. "Anybody with eyes could tell you've been getting gum from somewhere. Get ready to share the wealth 'cause if I don't beat you, Gladys will."

"Two against one ain't fair," Lucille muttered. "Don't forget I'm only four."

"Four going on twelve, and I'm not playin' against you, honey," Gladys said. "I play for myself. You'll be five in six months so quit feelin' sorry for yourself. I'm not an easy touch."

"It ain't fair bein' the only kid around here," Lucille grumbled. "Why don't you and Mr. Sterling get married? We could use a baby."

"Hush yourself up Lucille," Estelle said. "It isn't proper to talk like that. Do you two want that ace of spades? 'Cause I'll buy it if you don't."

"I need it and it's my turn so maybe you can use this," Gladys said as she discarded a nine of hearts. "I ain't getting married 'till I'm through school. And then I'm not having babies. Too much work."

"I thought all married people had babies," Lucille blew a bubble and discarded the king of hearts.

"Lucille, this conversation isn't any of your business. It's private. Now hush up before I wash your mouth out with soap. I'll buy that," Estelle said and glared at Lucille.

"Okay. It's your turn, Ma, you don't have to buy it," Lucille looked back innocently.

Estelle grabbed the card.

"I don't mind, Estelle, really," Gladys said as she drew a card from the deck and discarded a two of diamonds. "Lucille, babies should come when parents are ready to love and take care of them, not before. You're lucky to have folks who love you. My pa sent me to live here because he didn't like me."

"I'm sorry, "Lucille said chewing her gum. "I ought to mind Ma better and shut my mouth."

"Yes you should," Estelle muttered. "I'll buy that."

"Go ahead Ma, I don't need it," Lucille said and adjusted her cards and drew from the deck. "I've never met your pa."

"He isn't much like your Daddy, he's not nice," Gladys said. "I'll buy that."

"Go ahead," Estelle said. "Now, Miss Nosy Lucille, if you're done inquiring about things, let's get serious about this game."

"Alright Ma, Daddy always says you know best," Lucille said.

"Smart man, your daddy," Gladys said. "Rummy and pay up both of you. Next hand, two books and two runs."

# Chapter Twenty-six | Sunday Surprise
*Early Fall 1927*

"Bout time." Lucille bounced up and down on her toes and yelled at Sterling.

"We was gettin' ready to go into Sunday School without you. Lemme have a dime for the Sunday school offerin'. I forgot to ask Daddy, and Gladys didn't bring any money." Scowling at her aunty and holding out her hand she continued, "If we bring our Bibles and offerin' every Sunday and know our memory verse, we get three stars plus one for attendance. I aim to win the prize and I'm already ahead of everybody else."

"As long as you give for the right reasons," Sterling said drily and flipped her two nickels.

Lucille caught the coins in the air and started tucking one in her sock.

Gladys rolled her eyes and warned, "Don't be like Anannias and Saphiria and keep one for yourself."

"You mean those two people who got struck down dead because they cheated God out of his rightful portion?" Lucille asked, digging in her sock.

"That's right and you were about to do the same thing," Gladys admonished. "Your Mama would be heartbroken if you didn't make heaven on account of a candy bar."

"Well, I don't want to get struck dead and even though heaven don't sound like much fun, I'd rather go there than to where Satan lives with his demons. I'll buy a candy bar from my tips," Lucille skipped up the steps to the first and second grade room.

"Well, she certainly looks scared to death," Sterling observed.

"She's having problems adjusting to school, and Estelle wants to curb her unruly behavior." Gladys took Sterling's arm and they went up the steps to the sanctuary. "I'll fill you in this afternoon."

"Lil Sis is a pistol," Sterling laughed.

They sat in the pew behind Bud and Estelle. Mr. Johns prayed and instructed them to open their Bibles to Romans chapter three. Sunday School bored Sterling. As illiterate as he was in the Bible, he was convinced two months was too long to spend on the first three chapters of Romans. He wished it was acceptable to whittle in church. Usually Gladys brought her diary and wrote or drew pictures. Today she slipped her gloved hand into his.

After church and lunch, they took a walk by themselves. Lucille couldn't go because she was being punished. They meandered across Main Street towards their favorite tree covered neighborhood.

"So what's she done at school?" Sterling asked and blew a fairy dandelion her way.

"Lucille talks all the time and won't stay in her seat." She playfully swatted his arm. "She spent last Friday afternoon sitting on a bench, keeping an elm tree company. Estelle and Bud went in for a meeting with the teacher.

"She's probably bored, she's smart like you."

They crossed a street. "Well, she's something," Gladys laughed. "But, I'm better behaved. Estelle is helping her write letters this afternoon apologizing to her teacher and principal. She's smart, but to immature to really be in school. She already reads and knows arithmetic. We've all treated her like a little adult and I 'pect she wants the same treatment at school. She's been countin' cards since she was three."

"I swan, that girl... hold up and shut your eyes. " Sterling stopped abruptly. "I have a surprise."

Guiding her steps he asked, "What do you think?"

Gladys opened her eyes and mouth in surprise and stared at the cutest house she'd ever seen.

"Like it?"

"It's perfect, Sterling. Someday I want a house just like this with two front windows and a flower bed full of red geraniums," Gladys said. "Mama always had them on the front porch. The house looks like it's smiling with the windows and that pretty green door."

"And there's a porch swing," Sterling said and squeezed her hand. "I've always wanted to sit in one and enjoy the evenin' with my pretty girl."

They paused hand in hand and looked. Dreams crowded their hearts, but they kept quiet sensing the time wasn't right. They wandered a few more streets, but then came back to the smiling house.

Gladys jumped as a little woman ran down the front walk waving and yelling.

"Hey, you two come right up here and have some iced tea. I thought you'd be back. Mr. Vaughn, and I've been waitin'."

She turned and bustled up the front porch, pointed to the swing and poured them big glasses of iced tea.

"I'm sorry, I'm confused." Gladys said as she took the tea and sat down.

"I took a wagon load of furniture to the depot for Miss Lessie on Thursday and she told me she needed to let this house." Sterling pushed the swing with his foot.

"I need a family to take care of this house until my husband and I decide what to do." Miss Lessie continued, "The railroad moved us here and then right after we bought this house they transferred him back to the City. I've been traveling back and forth, but it's not practical to keep two homes."

She eyed them curiously as she filled their glasses. "You two getting married soon or just courtin'?"

Gladys blushed and Sterling said, "Courtin'."

"Gettin' married soon?"

"No, not yet." Sterling took a sip of tea. "The house would be for Gladys and her family. They need a bigger place."

"My brother owns the Katy Café on Main." Turning to Sterling Gladys said, "You've already talked to Bud, haven't you?"

"Yes, and they're waitin' to see the house with you."

"I planned to list the house tomorrow," Miss Lessie explained. "But, if your folks want it, I'll knock five dollars off the first month's rent. And you can move in this week."

Gladys grabbed her hand. "I'll be right back with Bud and Estelle. I'm sure you have a lovely home." She dropped Miss Lessie's hand, "C'mon Sterling, let's go get Bud and all them."

And without saying goodbye, Gladys took off her good shoes, sprinted down the walk and ran towards home.

"Heh, heh," Miss Lessie snorted, "you better get goin' or you won't catch up with that girl."

Sterling nodded. "Thank you for waitin' to rent the house. She's been sleepin' in the kitchen of the café and Bud wants to get the girls settled in a house."

"Give me a half hour to tidy up and make more tea before you bring them around."

Sterling opened the door for her and then ran after Gladys.

Miss Lessie and Bud agreed to twelve dollars a month. They moved in a week later on a Saturday afternoon. Gladys and Lucille shared a bedroom and Bud and Estelle took the slightly larger room. In the bathroom, Lucille couldn't get enough of the pull chain toilet and big claw foot tub. Finally, Estelle told her to stay out unless she was with her or Gladys.

Sterling moved out of the hotel and into the newly vacated backroom in the rear of the Katy. He brewed the coffee in the morning and opened the place before Bud and Estelle got there to handle the rush. They gained an extra half hour of sleep and spent a few minutes with the girls before school.

A spare bed was kept made and waiting for Jack in the dining room. It sat in an alcove intended for a buffet or wardrobe. They ate in the kitchen or at the café. Bud wrote to Pa and asked if he would send Jack.

Pa agreed Jack could come. Daisy was expecting another baby and had no room for the two of them. Pa wanted to go back to Leedey and live in the sod house on his land, but by the cemetery. He gave Jack the choice of living with him or moving to Elk City. Jack chose Elk City. In addition, Pa wanted an extra five dollars a month. Gladys felt it was a small price to pay for Jack's freedom. She and Bud agreed to a 50/50 split. Their money, along with Pa's old age pension, would give him enough to live on.

"My dream's coming true," Gladys said to Sterling one evening as they sat in the swing. "In a couple of days, with Jack here, we'll all be a real family."

Sterling nodded and squeezed her hand and hoped that being a real family included him.

# CHAPTER TWENTY-SEVEN | JACK COMES

*March 1928*

The insistent knocking drew Gladys out of her daydream as she fried up a mess of bacon, sausages and potatoes on the grill. Bud got up from the counter to see who was at the door a half hour before opening.

"Probably some tin can tourist who don't know we don't open until seven on Saturday," he said. Unlocking the door he paused and then started clapping a tall young man on the back. "Well I'll be Henry T. Ford, Jack."

"Jack," Gladys ran around the counter and flew at her little brother who was as tall as she was. "You're here. I can hardly believe it."

She scanned his face looking for the boy of her memory. At twelve, Jack was lanky with a crop of peach fuzz on his upper lip.

"Believe it," Jack grinned. "I got Pa settled and hopped the freight this morning. He's snug as a bug, in the soddy. He's glad to be by Ma and the rest."

"That sounds nice. I gotta get back, smells like my potatoes are burning. Catch up later?" Gladys flipped the slightly burnt potatoes over and cracked eggs. Bud poured Jack a cup of coffee and three more for the train crew.

Jack carried a pillowcase with his belongings. He wore overalls, worn boots and a cowboy hat. He took a seat at the counter and added milk to his coffee.

The crew trudged in wiping their coal smeared faces with red handkerchiefs.

"Breakfast on the house today boys for giving my kid brother a lift from Leedey," Bud said.

"If I had known that scallywag was your brother, I would've invited him to sit with us in the cab," the engineer said and nodded to Jack. "Saw you hop on."

Jack smiled angelically and saluted with his coffee cup.

"He's living with us now," Gladys flashed them a smile. "How'll you all have those eggs?"

"Scrambled.

"Scrambled."

"Sunny side up."

Gladys cracked and whisked their eggs and set food in front of Jack. Completing the orders, Bud served the crew. She helped herself and sat down.

Bud told jokes and kept the coffee cups filled. He didn't expect the market day crowd for another twenty minutes and Estelle and Lucille would be arriving soon. Sterling had already left town for his road construction job.

"Daisy's as bad as ever. She nags all the time," Jack told Gladys shoveling a whole sausage in his mouth and continuing in a high voice. "'Clean up after Pa. Did you milk the cow? Do the dishes.' I'm glad to be outta there."

Suddenly he sat up and quizzically looked at his sister, "I've been so busy eatin' I didn't notice how different you look. What'd you do to your hair?"

Gladys patted her bob and anxiously said, "I straightened it. Do you like it this way?"

"Do you?" Jack asked.

"Yes I do. People see me now and not my hair."
She checked the biscuits and looked up as the bell attached to the door rang and Estelle and Lucille walked in. Bud met them at the coat rack and Estelle nodded and smiled in Jack's direction.

"Mornin' Ma'am."

Jack's eyes darted between Estelle and Gladys unsure of his reception. Gladys smiled and he extended his hand and said, "I hope I don't put you out much."

Estelle noted that he favored Bud, ignored his hand, and gave him a hug. "I'm sure you won't be any trouble and we're glad to have you. Call me Estelle."

Putting on her apron she called, "Lucille come and meet your uncle and eat."

Lucille stomped over and looked up at Jack.

"Hi," he said.

Gladys heard Lucille say, "I have a pet chicken and we ain't never gonna eat it. Her name is Henri. I have a swing and a lasso at my house. Do you wanna come over? I like gum and chocolate bars. Mama, can I drink my milk by this big boy?"

Ignoring Lucille, Jack got up and dumped his dishes in the sink. "I'm gonna take a look around town."

And he did his own stomping.

Gladys frowned and looked at Bud.

"Suit yourself," Bud shrugged.

Jack slammed the door on the way out.

"Well I never," Estelle muttered under her breath. "He doesn't seem much like you two. C'mon Lucille." Sitting down she patted a seat, "You can drink your milk by me."

"Mama, do you think that big boy wants to go to the picture show? Tom Mix is on every Saturday and the Lone Ranger." Lucille shoveled some egg in her mouth and continued. "I always get popcorn and pop and share with Stewie. Nobody cares that we sit in the balcony. We stuff popcorn in our overalls. I love my overalls."

"We know about Stewie," Estelle took Lucille's face and turned it towards her own. "Listen to me, I want you to give Jack time to settle in before you talk his ear off or take him to the movies. Understand?"

"Yes, Mama."

Estelle got up to help as more customers walked into the Katy.

"Finish that biscuit and if you want tips, start drying those dishes."

"Okay, Mama."

Gladys cooked, Estelle kept the biscuits and coffee flowing, Bud manned the cash register, cleared places and washed dishes. Lucille dried and put glasses and silverware on the low shelves.

"Sterling working towards Texas today?" Estelle asked Gladys.

"Yep, he left early on Beauty and rode a few miles out. He's gonna have to catch a ride as they go further West." Wrinkling her nose, she continued. "I'm surprised Jack shed us so quickly. I thought he would've hung around to visit."

"I was surprised myself. He's had a lot of changes the past few days." Estelle scraped the grill.

"I guess," Gladys said and prepared the sandwich board for lunch.

Around eleven the café emptied and they sat down for a quick five minutes. The door opened and Jack came in and sat down.

"Did you have a nice walk?" Gladys asked.

"Nice town. Not as big as the City. Looks like a lot of gas stations are getting built now that the 66 is gonna go through. Maybe I can get a job pumpin' gas."

"I thought you were going to help out here." Gladys said.

"Sure," he grinned. "What can I do?"

"Lucille, teach Jack how we do dishes and he can do them during lunch while you and Stewie go to the movies." Estelle replied firmly.

Lucille brought her step stool over and began instructing Jack on the finer points of dishwashing.

"We scrape the plates into the trash and then wash dishes in the first sink." Pointing to the second sink, "This one is for bleach water. We add two caps of bleach. The third sink is to rinse the bleach and then dishes dry on this rack." She patted the flat space to her left that held a strainer and dishes that were drying.

"The dishes and glasses go underneath the counter except for the plates which go up by the grill," Lucille grabbed two glasses and stowed them away.

Jack watched her with a bemused expression as she efficiently took plates from the rinse water and stacked them on the empty strainer. He looked over at Gladys who winked at him and mouthed "later" to him. She never could stay mad at Jack.

"Okay Lucille," Jack said. "I guess you're the boss. How old are you anyways?"

"I'm five and do you like to read?" Lucille asked and flicked some suds at him.

"Not much," Jack replied flicking her back. "But I play the harmonica."

After the lunch rush Estelle sent Jack and Gladys off by themselves. Gladys took Jack to the house.

They walked into the dining room. "We never eat in here and this is your room. Your bed is private here by the window. You can draw the drapes back and get plenty of air and pull these pocket doors closed and nobody will bother you. When we lived at the Katy we didn't have much privacy. I like the house better and its fun sharing a room with Lucille instead of sleeping in a kitchen."

"I'm happy not to be sleepin' with Pa and my bed's fine," Jack stretched out. "I'm tired. I never seem to sleep much."

He turned over and went to sleep.

"So much for a good chat," Gladys muttered and closed the pocket doors.

Sterling walked into the Katy dusty and hot from working the road. "I feel like I've been eating tar."

Bud slapped a burger on the grill and poured him a glass of tea. Sterling gulped it down and poured himself another.

Sterling emptied the dishwater and put a bucket in the sink and began drawing water for his washing up in the backroom. Estelle sat at the counter. Bud leaned against the wall worrying a toothpick. The café was empty.

"Jack's here," Bud said.

Sterling turned off the water and straightened up, "You don't say, Gladys must be happy."

"We sent them home for the afternoon to get reacquainted," Estelle said. "It's been four years since they saw each other. I expected him to be more excited to see her." She pulled at her lip. "Something about the boy worries me, but I want him to feel welcome."

She removed her apron and Bud slid a hamburger and fries in front of Sterling.

"Think you boys can handle things for the next hour? I want to make that boy a cake, maybe soften him up."

"You go on, Kid." Bud said. "It's dead as Grant's tomb in here anyway."

Estelle walked to the movie house and waited for Lucille. Lucille chatted and skipped her way home. They met Gladys in the kitchen up to her elbows in potato salad. Two cake layers cooled on the window ledge,

"How's he doing?" Estelle asked Gladys looking around at Gladys' handiwork.

"Honestly, I don't know," Gladys replied and washed and dried her hands on the dishtowel embroidered with a bluebird. "My old Jack never would've taken off to see the town without visiting with his kin folk."

"Don't read too much into the first few days," Estelle said.

Lucille tugged at her mama's dress.

"Can I go swing?" she asked.

"Sure honey."

Estelle and Gladys spent a quiet quarter hour cooking before Bud and Sterling appeared.

Sterling kissed her cheek, "I'm glad Jack is here. Brothers and sisters ought to be together."

His voice got husky and his eyes soft, "I missed my sister something fierce when we were separated from each other on the orphan train. The family that chose her didn't want a boy and I kept riding 'til I got picked by an ol' boy who needed help on his farm."

"I would like to hear about that sometime," Gladys leaned against him smelling his soap and enjoying the feel of his body. He always felt like home.

"I'm glad Beth Anne lived here," Bud said. "And you all spent time together 'fore she got married and moved."

"She was the first person I met at the school." Gladys remarked. "She was so nice to me and let me hide in the closet to take all the entrance tests."

Smiling, Sterling said, "She told me about that and liked you a lot. By the way, anything we can do for Jack?"

"I don't know, but I would like to do for him like what you all did for me." Gladys nodded at Bud and Estelle. "He probably wants to pick out his own underwear, though."

"You're never going to give me any peace about that," Estelle said with an exaggerated sigh, as she put the bottom layer of the cake on a plate.

"No doubt," Bud replied. "Estelle and I don't mind helpin', but I know you feel responsible for him."

"Just take it slow, Gladys. You were ready to have us to help," Estelle warned. "He's young and wants to do things his way."

"That's good advice and a car ride is a sure cure for orneriness. How about we take him out tomorrow and he can see the countryside?" Sterling suggested.

"After church would be perfect," Estelle said. "I'll pack a picnic and we can eat by the creek."

"Good idea, Kid," Bud said. "C'mon Sterling. Let's see if the livery has a car available. Back in about an hour?"

"Supper will be on the table," Estelle said.

Gladys left and peeked through the pocket doors to find Jack setting up the old checker set.

"So you brought that with you?"

"Wanna play?" He asked. "

"Sure," Gladys replied with a sigh of relief and asked, "feeling better?"

"Some," he said.

# Chapter Twenty-eight | Trouble

*Spring 1928*

Gladys walked around the school to the junior high side to wait for Jack. The glittering late afternoon sun hurt her eyes and she moved into the shade of an oak tree. The new growth sprouted baby leaves that shuddered in the spring breeze. Jack walked right past her as he kicked the ground and muttered to himself.

"Hey Jack," she called and caught up with him. "Why so glum?"

"Don't want to talk about it."

Dodging other students leaving school and ignoring his wishes, Gladys continued her questioning,

"C'mon you used to tell me everything, but lately you've been as closed mouthed as Pa."

"That's a cheap shot," he retorted, pulled a cap from his back pocket and shoved it angrily on his head so it covered his eyes.

They stopped in front of Lucille's school to wait. Jack stuffed his hands in his pockets and leaned against a light post and wouldn't look at Gladys. The bell rang and after a few minutes Lucille came skipping out with the other second graders. She yelled bye to her friends, ran over, and started waving a paper in front of her aunt and uncle.

"Look at my paper; I got an A plus on my spelling test. Miss Parker says I gotta take spelling with the third graders, I'd rather be a second grader, but if I talk back I gotta sit under that dumb tree and can't talk to any kids for the rest of the day."

"Good for you, choosing the lesser of two evils," Gladys said and gave her niece a hug.

"What does that mean?" Lucille asked and handed her book bag to Gladys and buttoned up her sweater.

"It means you made the right choice."

"Good. I'll spell with the big kids," Lucille said. "They like me anyways."

"At least one of us is smart," Jack muttered as they rounded the last corner.

Gladys shot him a look. "Huh?"

"You wanna listen to the radio with me tonight, Jack?" Lucille asked.

Jack shook his head no.

They walked quickly home and entered the unlocked back door off the kitchen. Estelle had left fresh sugar cookies on the table. Jack grabbed a handful, went to his room and slammed the doors shut. Gladys opened the icebox and retrieved the bottle of milk. Lucille put the glasses on the table.

"Why's his panties in a bunch?" Lucille asked and dunked a cookie in a glass of milk.

"Underwear, only girls wear panties and I dunno what's wrong," Gladys got up to get a glass of water. "But I think he doesn't like something about school."

"Me, too," Lucille said. "I don't like getting in trouble all the time for talkin'."

"Wipe your mouth," Gladys said and handed her a dish towel. "But you don't get in trouble half as much as you used to. I think your deportment is improving."

"That's true!" Lucille smiled and put her dishes in the sink. "I'm gonna change clothes and go swing."

Gladys looked out at the tire Bud had hung in the backyard. "You do that. Any homework?"

"Naw, I finished it in school." Lucille ran to their bedroom and then ran outside.

Gladys put her dishes in the sink and turned the oven on to cook the meatloaf and vegetables Estelle had prepared that morning. She sat down at the kitchen table and worked on Algebra.

The door to the dining room slid open and Gladys looked up. She watched Jack open the fridge and drink the last of the milk out of the bottle. His eyes were swollen and red.

"You want to talk yet?"

"I guess I better," Jack said, "before Bud gets home."

He still didn't look at her but swallowing hard he went on to explain. "I don't like it here. School's hard and I don't like Estelle 'cause she's as bossy as Daisy. All of you do what she says like she's a queen and I can't do what I want. I had more freedom with Pa. I made money and was my own boss."

"Jack I'm surprised. I thought you wanted to be together as a family, but all you want is money?" Gladys said and glanced out the window at Lucille swinging up to the darkening sky.

"No, that's what you wanted." Jack continued. "I can't take the confinement. I care for you, but not much for anybody else. I would've stayed with Pa, but I couldn't make enough money. Pa didn't care if I didn't make it to school so I worked odd jobs and gave him what he thought was half. If I stayed out of his way, we got along."

Jack smiled, "Daisy nagged, but I smacked her boys if they said anything, made sure I was always home for dinner."

"You're kidding," Gladys raised her voice in astonishment. "Why didn't you say something before this?" Bewildered she continued, "after Pa beat me and whipped you, you still smacked her boys?'

"They're brats, like Lucille," he said simply.

"You take that back!" Gladys seethed. "She's not a brat and you better not touch her."

"Tell her to leave me alone and quit askin' me to do stuff," Jack hollered back. "I ain't playin' with no baby. He pulled up his shirt, "Do you see any titties?"

"Shut your mouth." Gladys shouted, "Ma would've washed your mouth out with soap for saying that word!"

"Grow up, Gladys!" Jack yelled and banged the back door as he left. Running over to the tire swing he gave it a savage push before trotting through the neighbor's yard.

Lucille screamed in delight, but Gladys ran outside.

"Hey," she yelled at Jack. "Leave her alone."

"What a jackass," she muttered.

Jack didn't come home for dinner. While they ate, Lucille wondered where he was and chattered about her day. She excused herself and went to listen to radio shows in the parlor.

Gladys looked at Bud and Estelle. All she had wanted was to give Jack a chance of a good life. The same kind of life they had provided for her.

"What's botherin' you?" Bud asked. "Somethin' about Jack?"

"Yes, he coulda hurt Lucille real bad today," she said softly. "He was mad and went by and pushed her swing. She almost fell off, but she thought he was playing with her. We got in a big argument, and he told me he used to hit Daisy's boys and threatened harm to Lucille if she didn't leave him alone."

With a catch in in her throat she said softly, "I'm afraid for Lucille and I don't know who this Jack is."

Bud got up from the table and looked out into the yard. It was almost dark.

"I'm goin' for a walk," he said and closed the back door.

Gladys looked over at Estelle and noticed the color had drained from her face. Her lips were set in a grim line and she was white around the mouth.

"This is too much." Estelle cleared her throat and said, "We got a call from school today. He's not turning in any assignments and refuses to take tests. I thought he needed time to settle in, but maybe he's doing this on purpose. He knows we won't tolerate meanness towards Lucille."

"What're we gonna do?" Gladys dabbed her eyes with an apron and began clearing the table. "He's changed so much."

"Life is going to have to teach him," Estelle brushed Gladys' hair from her face and pulled her back to the table. She poured tea for both of them and explained. "He's angry and needs to figure out what he wants. That is something you can't do for him."

"I know," Gladys said. "But what about him and Lucille? Shouldn't he apologize?"

"Lucille thinks he was playing with her," Estelle said simply. "Let's keep it that way. Besides, Bud will handle it."

They were washing and drying the dishes when the back door opened and Bud came in holding Jack by his jacket.

"I'm sorry for missin' dinner and being mean," Jack mumbled. His eyes were hidden and he wouldn't look at them. "I'll get my things."

"What's going on?" Gladys asked as he disappeared.

"Leave him alone, Gladys," Bud said. "He'll come around when he's ready. I've had a talk with Sterling and if Jack's so fired up to make money and being a man, he can start shoveling asphalt. Sterling's gonna mind him for a while, and I hope, work him half to death or at least 'till he's not quite so onery."

Jack came back in wearing overalls, boots and his old cowboy hat. His things were shoved in the old pillowcase. He went over to Gladys and pushed the hat up so he could see her. She searched his eyes and hoped to catch a glimpse of her old little brother.

"I guess you're right," he nodded. "I got more of Pa in me than I thought."

He glanced around the warm kitchen and followed Bud down the back steps into the darkness.

*Dear Diary,*

*Jack left today. He's living with Sterling. I hope Sterling can set him to rights. My heart can't take losing him.*

*Gladys*

# CHAPTER TWENTY-NINE | MILESTONES

*June 1929*

The day dawned hot and cloudless. Outside of town, the broomcorn and wheat grew lush and green. Route 66 snaked west of Elk City and the men working the road hoped to merge with the east bound Shamrock Texas highway later in the summer. They were hopeful of quitting early to attend the high school graduation ceremony.

At the newly built pool in the park, Jack straightened the chairs and hosed off the concrete. Some of the younger members of town stood in a line along the chain link fence waiting for morning swim lessons followed by an afternoon of swimming. Tomorrow, Saturday, the colored kids would swim in the afternoon before the pool was drained, scrubbed, and filled for Monday.

Jack sprayed the line to delighted shrieks.

"Kid stuff," Jack muttered as he finished. He didn't have time to swim. Maintaining the pool was one of his jobs. He also worked at the Sinclair filling station and any other job he could find. He was known around town as a handy sort, even if he was young. He hustled in hopes of owning his own station and garage someday further west. Batching with Sterling suited him just fine, working the road had not. He paid for his half of the room and was left alone.

After his argument with Gladys last winter, they'd come to an uneasy peace. She'd made him promise to attend her graduation. He'd go if it was convenient.

Gladys and Lucille were sleeping when Estelle checked on them before work. From the parlor, she brought a fan to circulate the air. Both girls were red cheeked from spending the day at the pool yesterday. Lucille looked hot and mussy. She insisted on sleeping in her cowboy pajamas year-round. She coughed and turned over. Her light brown curls were as tousled as her bedclothes. On the other hand, Gladys looked neat as a pin with the sheet up to her neck. She lay on her back with a pillow jammed under her neck and her hair rolled up in soup cans. Waunetta had relaxed her roots a week ago in anticipation of graduation

Her peach dress hung on the door of the wardrobe. It was dotted Swiss and a nosegay of artificial roses lay on the dresser to be pinned at her waist. Lucille's new outfit dangled from the doorknob, a Dale Evans cowboy shirt and skirt. Estelle tiptoed out of the room and left the door open.

Bud waited for her on the front porch. He sat in the rocking chair with his long legs stretched out in front of him and his cowboy hat on his lap.

"Girls sleepin'?" he asked as Estelle bustled out. He got up, locked the front door, and took her hand.

"Like rocks. They're worn-out from swimming yesterday. Gladys wore a big hat and a scarf so her hair wouldn't get splashed and Lucille's part mermaid. Gladys caught her swimming through people's legs and told her she could only go through legs that belong to ladies. Lucille wanted to know why and Gladys told her to ask me. We had a little talk last night on proper pool etiquette. I told her she can't go swimming today anyway because I want her rested for graduation. She was up half the night barking with that cough."

"I heard. All kids get the croup. So what are those two doin' instead?"

"Gladys is planning on egg facials and painting their fingernails. She's going to wash and style Lucille's hair."

"Sounds lovely," Bud intoned. "Think we'll see them around lunchtime?"

"They'll have to. Not much to eat in the house. Lucille wants her fried baloney and Gladys could live on tuna fish sandwiches. Not to change the subject, but what did Sterling want with you last night?"

"He asked my permission to give Gladys a ring.'

"Really," Estelle remarked, not at all surprised. "Seems appropriate with her graduating and starting training. He's been respectful to her and our wishes."

"He told me he was willin' to wait until she completes her nurses trainin'." Bud continued. "They've got a few wrinkles to work out with him dead set on bein' a rancher and she's just as set against it."

"If any two people can figure it out, they will," Estelle opened the door to the Katy. "Looks like our regulars have helped themselves to Sterling's coffee. I'm thankful he brews that big pot before work."

"Does save us some trouble. Mornin' all," Bud called, and Estelle nodded and prepped the grill.

Customers called their orders to Estelle and she repeated them back and prepared the food. Bud ran hot water in the sinks, made more coffee and refilled cups as he joked and greeted everyone by name.

"So, your Gladys is graduating tonight?" Mr. Jones, the druggist, remarked to Bud as he refilled his coffee. "My Hope is too, and then we're planning on seeing all of you at her wedding tomorrow."

"We wouldn't miss it," Estelle said as she brought him his breakfast. "I need to drop by the drugstore later to pick up something for Lucille. She crouped most of last night, so I dapped her throat with turpentine and had her drink whiskey, honey and lemon juice."

"That's usually a good remedy and knocks the kids and the cough right out." Mr. Jones got up to leave. He only drank coffee in the morning. "Tell you what, I'll call Doc and see if he'll recommend something stronger."

"I'd appreciate it," Estelle said. "Coffee's my treat today."

"It's probably from swimmin' in that durn pool," Mr. Madison interjected from further down the counter. "I told Patsy to keep our kids out of it and to swim in the creek."

"How's Patsy feeling these days?" Estelle asked hoping to avoid an argument. She had a low opinion of Mr. Madison.

"Poorly. My oldest girl, Bertha helps her, but we've got one of our own now and she's expectin' again." He shoveled egg in his mouth and dribbled a good part down the front of his overalls. "Gladys and Patsy were good friends in school. Tell her to come see Patsy sometime. Do her some good."

"I'll tell her, but she starts nurse's training in a week." Estelle cleared the counter and dumped dishes in the sink. "My goodness, two kids for Patsy in two years and your other three from Hannah. That girl must be worn to a frazzle."

"She's young and strong and knew what she was takin' on when we was married." Mr. Madison responded hotly. "Besides, I wouldn't let any wife or girl of mine do somethin' as foul as nursin'. She ain't colored or Catholic or a low woman. If you and Bud had any sense, you'd marry her off."

"Well good thing some of us loose women were around to help with Hannah before she died." Estelle retorted pointing a soapy spatula at him. "Things have changed and for Pete's sake, this is the twentieth century the last time I looked at my calendar. Gladys makes up her own mind. Low woman, my foot. "

Bud put a hand on her shoulder and gently walked her to the grill and took over talking.

"Mr. Madison when my sister was eleven she nursed and watched our mama, sister and brother die from typhoid. She's planned on being a nurse ever since and we're proud of her being the first of our family to graduate high school and live to tell about it."

"Women need to stay at home," Mr. Madison retorted and flipped three cents on the counter. "I quit school when I was ten."

"And it shows," Estelle muttered and wiped her face with her apron.

"Look what that cat drug in," Bud said as Gladys and Lucille wandered in right before lunch wearing overalls, curlers and scarves. "You two are a sight."

"Daddy, we ain't cats," Lucille croaked. "We're gettin' beautiful for graduation."

"She's got that barky cough still," Gladys remarked. "I gave her some of your cough syrup Estelle, but it didn't help."

Lucille sat down at the end of the counter and lay her head on her folded arms.

Estelle retrieved a small bottle from under the counter and poured Lucile a teaspoonful. She sat down and held Lucille in her lap.

"Mr. Jones brought this concoction over this morning. It's stronger. Now, you two sit down and eat and then go home and rest."

"'Kay Mama," Lucille drank it down. "Nasty."

"You feel hot, Sweetie."

Gladys finished preparing their sandwiches and sat down next to them and took a big bite from her sandwich.

"I made a lemon pie this morning for after graduation."

"Mama, I ain't hungry." Lucille pushed her plate away. "I'm sleepy."

Estelle felt her forehead, again.

"You're feverish."

"I'll take her home." Gladys jumped up and reached under the counter for wax paper and wrapped the sandwiches. "C'mon Lucille, I'll give you a piggyback ride."

Lucille reluctantly stepped on a red stool and wrapped herself around Gladys.

"Come home, Mama."

"I will as soon as I can. Here, Honey, take this bottle of Bubble-Up."

When they got home, Gladys dosed Lucille with two cherry flavored aspirin. She ran a cool tub and then tucked her in for a nap. She left the door open and angled the fan so it did not blow directly on her niece but cooled the room. Slipping her feet underneath her she wrote:

June 14, 1929

Dear Diary,

Tonight, I graduate. Nursing school begins in a week.

Lucille has the croup and is running a fever. I wouldn't let her wear her cowboy pajamas to take a nap and she didn't even fight me. This is worrisome.

I see Jack around town, but I'm kept at arm's length.

Sterling bought a new suit and looks so good. Tomorrow we're going to Clinton for dinner and a dance. I'm wearing my graduation dress. We haven't seen each other much lately because we've been so busy.

I hope he gives me the ring we picked out. I can't wait till we're engaged. It seems stupid that they only want unmarried women in nursing school.

In a way I'm scared to love him too much. God forbid, but what if something happens to him?

Lucille's coughing again. I'm gonna check on her.

Gladys

P.S. I don't mind hard work, just farm work. Sterling and I gotta figure this out.

# Chapter Thirty | Diary Entries
*Summer 1929*

*July 7, 1929*
*Dear Diary,*

*I feel so stupid writing Dear Diary. What does a book know about life? I think I should title my entries, dear earlier me.*

*Almost three weeks ago, I graduated. That same night, Lucille ran a high fever and had a seizure. We were all frantic. The doctor wanted her in the hospital, but Estelle convinced him she could take care of her. I wanted to forget about school and stay home and help, but she wouldn't hear of it and said I wouldn't get this chance again.*

*Lucille has rheumatic fever and it's gone to her joints and perhaps has affected her heart. Only Estelle tends her because she's contagious.*

*So Sterling quit the 66 and helps Bud run the café. When it gets busy, the regulars pitch in and pour coffee and wash dishes.*

*I feel so numb inside. It's like when Mama came down with typhoid and I coped by not feeling things. I was so busy with cooking, laundry and cleaning up. I was a machine doing what needed to be done. Then after Ma and all them died, Pa beat me. I don't know how I would've survived without Bud and Estelle.*

*I'm that machine again, working sixteen hours a day either studying or on the ward. Since I don't have time to wash and iron my uniform, Sterling insisted I send mine out to the laundry and he'd pay for it. That's a help because out uniforms and aprons have to be spotless at the beginning of the day.*

*Now that I'm in school I get every other Saturday afternoon off, and I can see Lucille then.*

*I've been in school four days and it seems like forever. Lucille is my niece, but she's also my friend. She's always bugging me for a Hershey bar and to play cards with her. My heart is being squeezed by an iron fist. I'll buy her a million candy bars if she just gets well.*

Sterling and I decided to wait to become engaged. He loves her as much as I do and is always calling her "Lil Sis." He chose a special gift for her when I get my ring. I miss seeing my folks every day.

On my afternoon off, I aim to cook some meals ahead and do what I can for Estelle to ease her and Bud's load. It's after ten and I got to get some sleep before 5:30.

July 15, 1929

Estelle sent a note today telling me that Lucille's fever broke but she still spikes a fever in the evening, but not as high.

Sterling sent me flowers and a note today telling me he needs to ask me something on my next Saturday afternoon off, because he wants all the doctors and orderlies to know I'm taken. Like he has anything to worry about from me!

I bet he sent Lucille a bouquet, too.

Lucille's Entries:

August 3, 1929

Dear Diary,

This is nuts. I'm stuck in this bed with this ol' roomatick fever. I started getting sick the day Gladys graduated and Mama and I had to stay home and miss all the fun. But it was okay because I was too sick to care and I almost died. I ain't never almost died before.

The doctor comes by to see me every day. Sometimes he gives me a shot to build me up. I hate shots.

Mama is the only one who can come in and see me. Everybody else has to holler at me through my bedroom door or window because I might make them sick. Both my knees are all swoll up and Mama lays hot packs on them and they don't ache so much. I gotta swallow water with melted aspirin; it's supposed to help, but it don't work and I cry, but it makes everybody feel bad.

*Gladys gave me this notebook for my diary. She told me to write or draw whatever I want and keep it shut with a rubber band. I wrote "Keep Out" on it with my red crayon and I hope Ma pays attention.*

*Sometimes Sterling slides me a candy bar across the floor. He's got a good aim and I hang upside down from my bed and retrieve it. I can color, but I ain't allowed to read yet or play cards. I can't even chew gum because I might choke. I like it when Daddy or Sterling read or talk to me through the window.*


*August 4, 1929*

*Dear Diary,*

*The best news is Gladys and me is engaged to Sterling. He proposed to Gladys first and now she wears a sticky up diamond ring called a solitaire. I thought solitaire was a card game, but it's a ring too. Then Sterling gave me a ring and jimmied the screen to put it on my finger. It's my January birthstone. He called it a garnet and asked me to be his forever niece. I said yes and told him I would hug him when Ma says I can. I ain't ever been engaged before.*

*Gladys don't come around much because she's so busy at nursing school and lives at the hospital.*

*I get a new Dale Evans outfit when I'm well. I can't even get out of bed and go pee or poop. I have to use a bedpan and if I get stopped up, Ma gives me an enema. I hate enemas.*

*I can't even sit up when Ma changes my sheets. I have to lie on a quilt on the floor like a baby. I watch her wipe down the plastic sheet that covers my mattress and then lots of old quilts go on top of that so I don't sweat. I sweat anyways. Then Ma puts on my sheets and top quilt. She gives me a sponge bath when I'm on the floor and lifts me back in bed. Sometimes I pretend Susie is sick and she gives her a bath, too. I hate sponge baths.*

*Here's a picture of my goat that Daddy bought so I can have fresh milk. The doctor said I have to drink a lot of it and Ma says now I smell like a little goat. I check my arms a lot to make sure I'm not starting to grow hair like a goat. I don't like the taste, but I get all the Hershey's syrup I want.*

*I'm tired and I'm going to take a nap. See you later diary!*

183

*August 11, 1929*

*Dear Diary,*

Gladys came by because she was running an errand for the hospital. She looks so pretty in her uniform. It's blue with a big white apron that's pinned to the front of her dress and tied in the back. She don't have a hat yet because she's a student nurse and ain't a real nurse. I told her I was okay and I want to hear about her graduation someday. She told me how I got rheumatic fever and I want to write it down before I forget how to spell it.

I got strep throat and got worse and now I have rheumatics fever. I have to be still so my heart don't get damaged. Sometimes at night my heart pounds like a freight train and I get scared. I asked Gladys if I could ever get out of my bed again and she said I can when my heart quits pounding and I don't have fevers. Then visitors can come see me as long as the doc says it's okay. I'm glad I won't be paralyzed or dead like polio. Then she had to go.

Here's Ma with some slimy custard. I wish I could have animal cookies instead. I hate custard.

Custard made out of goat milk is the worst.


*August 28, 1929*

Things are a mess around here. Daddy tied Nanny Goat to the clothesline in the backyard because the front yard is grazed clean from you know who. Nanny Goat ate Ma's best blouse right off the line. Ma fussed at daddy and yelled at Nanny Goat. In the meantime, Sterling and daddy dosed Nanny with castor oil and are hanging around for results. I saw the whole thing from my window. It's better than a picture show.

# Chapter Thirty-one | Goodbye Again

*1930*

Gladys hated to say goodbye again. Her whole life was one big goodbye. Goodbye to Ma, Clarence and she guessed Ivy and Pa. Goodbye too, to little boy Jack and hello to grown up strange Jack. Goodbye to the Katy Café and the warm memories. And now goodbye to the three of the five people she loved most in the world.

"Why don't you come with us Gladys?" Lucille pleaded with her. "We can ride in back and play gin rummy all the way to Arizona. It'll be so borin' without you. Who's gonna keep me company? Pa and Mama are gonna talk all the way there and I'll just be stuck."

"You know I can't leave Sterling or school right now, no matter how much I love you," Gladys said and wished her eyes would stop leaking. "As soon as we can, we'll be out to see you. You just have to get well."

"I'm tryin', don't cry. I got you a present." Lucille whipped two pairs of sunglasses out of her carpetbag and placed a pair on Gladys and one on herself.

Gladys cried harder and hugged Lucille

Bud came out of the house and pulling on his tan driving gloves, sized up the situation, "I think Lucille and me will go ahead and say goodbye to Jack and fill the car." Kissing his sister's wet cheek, he winked, "be back in a flash."

Drying her eyes and face with her sleeve, Gladys went in the house and stooped down to help Estelle finish wrapping plates in newspaper. "I can't believe this is happening again. Everyone I love gets sick or dies. Sterling ought to take off running and never look back."

Estelle took the plates from her and finished packing the dish box. She took her hand and walked to the porch swing. Sitting them both down she said, "Honey, this is a lot to take in right now for all of us. Everything has happened so fast. My own head is swirling, but truth be told, I'm looking forward to a change of scenery. Lucille's going to be okay; the doc says we just have to get her out of the dust and breathing clear air. If that doesn't help, Arizona has hospitals. We have money from the sale of the Katy and the three of us will be gypsies until we settle."

"I know. You make perfect sense, but I'm so scared for Lucille." Gladys pushed the sunglasses up on top of her head and wiped her eyes, again.

Estelle pushed the swing a bit with her feet and continued. "You have money in the bank, the hospital feeds and provides a place for you to sleep, and you have a good man. Don't let the fears of the past cloud the cheer you have now and hope for the future."

"But Lucille might die! How can you stand it?"

"I stand it by taking care of the people I love and I truly believe that girl is too feisty for anything to happen." Estelle hugged her hard. "Now get up and help me finish."

"I guess it's time to stand on my own two feet and not depend on you and Bud," Gladys replied, twisting the ring on her finger.

They moved into the bedroom and checked the room.

Glancing wistfully around, Gladys said, "I'm going to miss this house. You aren't leaving until Sterling gets here, are you?"

"Of course not. Bud and I love him like a brother, and it would be impossible to leave you, if he weren't here with Jack acting the way he is. How one kid can make himself so scarce in a small town is beyond me." Sweeping under the two beds she continued, "That's it in here. The new renters want the beds. Why don't you finish packing the trunk and I'll continue sweeping the house."

Gladys snapped the locks on the trunk, went to the porch and sat on the steps. Her thoughts circled back to her lonesome leaving of her home in Leedey when Pa sent her away. She waited and soon Bud and Lucille drove back with Sterling.

"Hey, Honey," Sterling called to her.

"Hey, Honey," Lucille mimicked. "How 'bout a kiss?"

"Get out of the car you little monkey and quit teasin' your aunt," Bud laughed and opened the door.

"Not a bad idea," Sterling said.

Gladys wrapped her arms around him and greeted him properly. "Soon it's just going to be us," she whispered.

"I know," he smiled. "You hang on to that thought, but right now I need to help Bud strap the trunk to the back of the car. When are you due back at the hospital?"

"Noon. My supervisor gave me the morning off. I'm working late tonight to make up the time."

"I'll see you Saturday then, wear something pretty."
"I will. Will we go dancing?"

"Count on it," and Sterling waltzed down the walk to help Bud.

Gladys laughed and danced with Lucille up the step, pretending to tap dance like in the movies. Lucille started coughing and Estelle stuck her head outside the door and reminded them that Lucille shouldn't exert herself.

"I hate this ol' fever. I ain't never gonna have any fun again," Lucille pouted.

"Oh yes you will. Your Ma assures me you'll be feeling fine soon, and I believe her."

The car was packed. Bud said there wasn't any extra room for a postage stamp. Estelle climbed into the seat next to Bud. Lucille sat high on a bed of quilts, eating marshmallow treats and drinking water from a clean mayonnaise jar. She waved to Gladys and Sterling and jammed her sunglasses on top of her head and started reading the stack of comic books they had given her as a going away present. Bud started the car and it lurched forward as Lucille's bicycle shuddered on top and they headed towards Arizona.

# Chapter Thirty-two | Letters between Arizona & Oklahoma

*1929 - 1930*

*November 3, 1929*
*Dear Gladys and Sterling,*

*Lucille is feeling better. The clear cold air of the Arizona Mountains agrees with her. We are settled in a pine forest and the air smells so nice.*

*Flagstaff is a pretty little college and lumber town. Bud works as a night watchman for the college and I cook in the cafeteria during the day. We are keeping Lucille home from school until she no longer runs a fever. She does her schoolwork with Bud and me on my days off.*

*We took her to a heart specialist in Phoenix. A valve in her heart is damaged and time will tell how badly. We are hopeful she will have as normal life as possible. I believe she's stronger. Bud and Lucille go on a walk every day and are enjoying getting to know everyone around town. Bud pulls her in a wagon when she gets tired, but she's walking a bit more every day. They watch the trains arrive and depart as the depot is right downtown.*

*We stopped in tourist camps along the way and Lucille thought it was fun. We blew a tire in Texas, and wanting to save the tires from then on, Bud nursed the car along at 30 miles per hour. It took over a week to get here. The mountain roads of New Mexico near about scared me to death. Some of the drops didn't have rails to keep you from dropping off. Lucille loved it and whooped and hollered. Every time we got going a little fast, I pulled up the emergency brake while Bud steered. I was a nervous wreck.*

*The car needs repair so here we're staying.*

*We had a lot of company on the road. You never saw so many cars. I'm glad they hired Sterling back on the 66 even if he does have to go farther out of town.*

*I'm sewing for extra money. One of my ladies has me sew for her niece and pays me in extra material so I can make nice clothes for Lucille.*

Bud bought me a Singer sewing machine since we had to sell my old one. If I could, I would stay home all day and sew.

I feel fortunate that we were able to start over without owing a cent. No denying that money is tight and barring any disasters we should be able to put a little away. We are renting a nice little house made of rocks. We have Lucille sleep in the living room because the wood stove keeps her warm. The bedroom is freezing so Bud and I took it.

Last Sunday, we ate dinner with a family from church. They have a daughter older than Lucille and those two are thick as thieves. Peggy plays cards as well, if not better than Lucille. She's learned new card games and can't wait to teach you one called of all things, Smut. We miss you, honey. Write soon and let us know how you are getting on. Give our love to Sterling.

Love,
Estelle

P.S. Hey Sis, Jack wrote me he's moving to Albuquerque. He got an offer to buy into a gas station and wants to borrow money. How's nurses' training going? Love, Bud

P.S.S. Hey Gladys, I made a friend named Peggy. She's teaching me how to play a lot of new games. I'm feeling better and I still ain't contagious. Write soon. Love, Lucille

November 20, 1929
Dear Estelle, Bud and Lucille,
I'm happy you made it to Arizona. Sterling says "hi." This is my half Saturday off and I'm sitting in the lobby at the new hotel. We're going to have dinner here later.

Sterling is looking through some papers he got yesterday from the bank. He's putting money down on a ranch. We drove out to see it today and I actually liked it, after he assured me he would hire a cook. I get butterflies imagining our life with a home of our own.

I didn't know Jack was planning a move. I never see him.

They moved all four of us student nurses to a big attic room because ours were needed for patients. We have a lot of fun together when we're not too tired.

Until the new nursing class starts, we have to wash the floors and disinfect the bathrooms and equipment. I'm faster than anybody else and so I also bathe a few patients. When I get married, I'm not going to be very surprised.

Sterling bought a used Ford pickup for the ranch. He's teaching me how to drive.

I don't have time to mess with my hair so I'm wearing it in a braid. Sterling likes my hair long and I like getting ready faster.

I'm using cornhusker's oil every night like you told me, Estelle. My cuticles are cracking, but not too bad. I do miss you all, but not as terrible as I thought.

Lucille, Sterling and I will come see you as soon as we're married, and you can teach me new card games and I will meet Peggy and her folks.

Gotta go. Love you all,

Gladys

January 4, 1930

Dear Estelle, Bud and Lucille,

Happy New Year! I hope you got the box we sent before Christmas. In my free time, I knitted you all something just from me. I know Sterling bought some surprises for Lucille, but I haven't seen him to find out what else he sent.

We're having our Christmas for each other tomorrow. I made him a muffler and bought him some leather gloves. We're saving your box till then.

I worked Christmas Eve and Day. We all did. It's awfully cold and we're having a lot of frost bite, pneumonia and flu. We can't do a lot for the elderly who are frail besides being so sick. We try to keep them warm and hydrated. I spent eight hours spooning warm broth into this one lady and she made it through the night. The next day her daughter took over, but she died anyway before midnight. We cried together as she remembered her ma and I remembered mine.

I go one day a week with Doctor Sahid and a senior nurse to provide care to the poor, mostly sharecroppers. Its first come, first served.

We take whatever people can afford as payment and usually go home with eggs, bacon, molasses and canned goods such as kraut or green beans. Doc Sahid knows it's important that people pay or trade something for care. He says for us to take what we want and I'm stocking Sterling's pantry. The rest we give to the hospital.

Dr. Sahid is from India and he started the hospital here. I like working with him, because he reminds me of Dr. Seavey.

Love,

Gladys


January 21, 1931

Hey Gladys,

I went to school and took a test. I could be a fifth grader if I was taller and older. I like Daddy teaching me better. I don't get in trouble. We study hard in the morning, eat sandwiches that Ma left and go on a walk in the afternoon. Or if it's too cold, we read stories and then nap. I don't bug Daddy after that because he works all night.

Ma says since I'm so smart I have to talk and write correctly. She borrows books for me from the library. I've read <u>Tom Sawyer</u> and <u>Huck Finn</u>. I'm starting <u>Little Women</u> and the librarian told Ma that Louisa May Alcott wrote a bunch of books and I get to read them all!

I'm beginning Algebra. I have a tutor come to the house twice a week. Ma's listening to the lessons and learning, too. She wants to get her high school diploma.

I ate some Mexican food. I had a taco and enchilada and Mr. Gabaldon is nice and the food was delicious. When you come, we're gonna eat there.

It's really cold and I don't get outside as much. When I do, I'm bundled like an Eskimo. They live at the North Pole and eat whale fat called blubber. Yuck!

I might get a dog. Peggy's dog had puppies and her ma had twins, a little girl and boy. The boy was born dead with a big head. Peggy don't see me as much because she's helping with the baby.

Love,
Lucille


March 8, 1930
Dear Folks,

I'm sure glad you're out of here. We've had a lot of blowing dust. It covers everything and everyone. Sterling says he's glad he's ranching and not farming. As long as he doesn't overgraze, he should be okay.

I was sorry to hear about Peggy's brother. Sounds like hydroencephalitis, which is water on the brain and is fatal.

Estelle, I'm happy you've decided to go back to school.

Gotta run.

Love, Gladys

Lucille, I loved all the Louisa May Alcott books!


Hello one and all,

I'm gonna tag onto this letter. I have ten head of cattle I'm running and I'm still working on the road. I mostly eat beans and eggs except when I'm in town.

The dollar is for Lucille for her and Bud to change into coins for the trains to run over.

My best,
Sterling

# CHAPTER THIRTY-THREE | LEEDEY, AGAIN

*Spring 1930*

> *April 1, 1930*
> *Dear Diary*
> *We buried Pa.*
>
> *He'd been living at the dugout by the cemetery all this time. He preferred it. I remember Ma always kept jars of peaches and greens as well as old quilts in case someone needed a place to stay.*
>
> *Daisy and I met at the funeral parlor to make arrangements. She's as bossy as ever and insisted on taking charge. If I cared more, I would have argued with her. Listening to Daisy it made sense why Pa preferred dead relatives to live ones; no one argues when you're dead.*
>
> *According to Doc Seavey, Pa'd come down with the flu. He tried to move him to a home for sick folks in town, but Pa wouldn't leave the dugout. Doc went to check on him and found him dead in bed. Said he looked peaceful.*
>
> *We're splitting the funeral bill four ways. Bud wired his and Jack's portion. Daisy squawked about paying so much, but I told her to pay up as Pa paid rent when he and Jack lived with her. I bet she's so tight she has to screw her skirt on in the morning.*
>
> *Sterling wanted to come with me, but I wouldn't let him. He can't afford to hire any hands yet and I can't see him getting behind on my account.*
>
> *I went and talked to Doc Seavey. I told him I'm in school to become a nurse and thanked him for encouraging me when Ma died. I remember one time Ivy got sick and lost control. Sick was everywhere and he helped me clean her up. Doc told me to go downstairs and get some sleep and he would watch. Instead, I stayed and he told me about doctoring during the war. I couldn't get enough of his stories.*
>
> *Doc took off his glasses and dabbed his eyes and said that it was the nicest thing anybody's said to him and that he always knew I was someone special.*
>
> *He turned around and took a small leather bag on a string off his neck. I wrote down what he told me verbatim.*

"I rode with the Calvary before the war. We tried to keep peace between the settlers who wanted to own land and the Indians who wanted to ride and live off the land. This bag was given to me by a Crow Medicine Man. A cholera epidemic was wiping out settlers and Indians alike. We worked side by side and learned from each other. When the situation eased, he gave me his medicine bag and told me never to open it because what's inside is sacred. In return, I gave him my Pa's pocket watch. I do believe the Great Spirit of the Plains heard my prayers a time or two when all other wisdom failed me." He finished by telling me, "Wear it if you like, but keep it safe. As healers we can't choose who we help and what god people follow."

I told him I would treasure the medicine bag always and asked him to come to my graduation.

We only had a graveside service. I brought flowers with me and remembered Ma and Clarence. Clarence will always be eight years old to me. I love Ma for making time to drink tea with me in the morning, even though she had eight mouths to feed. I put a flower on Ivy's grave because I knew I should.

On the drive back to Leedey from the cemetery, Daisy kept accusing me of being snooty because I graduated high school and I'm going to be a nurse. She thinks working in a mercantile is so much better. I told her to be still or I'd slap her. I'm done with sorry acting people.

I ride the train back tonight. I've missed Sterling and school. I'll have to work extra to make up for the day and a half I missed, but I don't mind. I'll see Sterling tonight when he picks me up. I can't believe it's only been six years since I left Leedey, a lifetime ago.

Gladys


July 23, 1930
Dear Diary,
It's been four months since I last wrote. My nose is about worn off by the nursing grindstone.
Bud, Estelle and Lucille are still doing well in Arizona and Lucille is better and breathing cleaner air.

*I spend my time off with Sterling. To save money we eat at the ranch with his hand Andy. I got to say running cattle is a heck of a lot more fun than farming. I never knew that taking care of calves, branding and separating a little bull from his dangly parts made for such a good time. Sterling's a bit worried that I like the blood and guts so much.*

*Last Saturday, we took a moonlight swim in the stock tank. I about lost my composure when we kissed under the stars. Afterwards, we agreed to swim from now on only in the daylight. Anyway, I am more than happy to sew up both man and beast when they need it. Sterling's not making much money yet, but he's having fun doing what he's always wanted. He and Andy run the outfit and trade off cooking. They don't like being called cowboys and I don't know why.*

*I like being there with him. It feels like home. I do like rocking in the porch swing and enjoying the evening colors and sounds. Sometimes we talk about what our life together will be like. Sterling understands things about me before I understand them myself.*

*What I love best about my Sterling is we never fight. We talk things out until we come to some sort of agreement that is satisfactory to both of us. Right now, we're discussing children. He wants a bunch and I don't. I don't know how I can be a nurse and raise a bunch of kids. Plus, you never know when times are going to get hard and you could lose your home or go hungry. No child of mine is going hungry. Neither one of us believes in whipping a child. He was whipped in the orphanage and then on the farm where he was adopted, and Lord knows I got my share. I'm not agreeing to anything about kids. He says he'll give me time to change my mind.*

*Bud and Estelle only have Lucille. They went to see a specialist a few years back and Estelle's insides aren't right after Lucille was born. You never know what's going to happen. Maybe you can be happy and lonesome for more kin at the same time.*


*August 1, 1930*
*Overall, I like the work of nursing, particularly now that we're experienced and get to take care of a carbuncle or a boil. I routinely assist with surgeries. Operations are fascinating. I've assisted with an appendix*

removal, hysterectomy and gall bladder, tonsils and adenoids surgery. I've watched anesthesia being administered, but to do it routinely requires more training than a two-year course. Folks don't come into clinic unless they're really sick. Sometimes we get a diphtheria, or polio case. I like the cases that the other girls don't want, because I know how much a smile and a confident touch can mean. Some of the medical staff treat the poor and sick people like lepers.

Treating the colored is voluntary. On Saturday mornings I go with Doc Sahid and another nurse to the garden shed. It's a clean room with an exam couch. We boil water in the yard and make do with clean old towels, sheets and supplies the hospital doesn't want. We set bones, inoculate; clean infected feet and anything else. We treat as fast as we can and get paid with live chickens or other food that we give to the kitchen or I take to the ranch. This is the best part of my nursing week, because I feel like I'm doing some real good.

Doc Sahid is himself colored, but people don't seem to notice because he speaks with a British accent. By law we can't treat colored people in the hospital, but he can treat a white man in the hospital. I don't get it.

My roommates are fun. Our attic is freezing in winter and boiling hot in summer. All four of us will graduate in June and we eat, sleep, study, and nurse patients together. Sometimes at night we talk and drink cokes. We send Tina down to the kitchen for ice because she's so quiet and little and can sneak in anywhere. Then we sit up and play cards or if it's really hot crawl out the window and onto the roof. We hide behind the dormers until we get so sleepy it's go inside or fall off the roof.

I've decided I want to be like Doc Seavey and Doctor Sahid. I'm going to take care of anybody who needs my help.

Gladys

# Chapter Thirty-four | Rusty Hills

*Late June 1931*

The screen door banged shut as Gladys maneuvered her way around the furniture on the porch with two steaming cups of coffee. The cicadas buzzed a greeting and a dust devil danced close to the cattle feeding in the far pasture.

"Sterling, come and get your coffee," she hollered, knowing he was in one of the out buildings surrounding the house. He stuck his head out of the bunkhouse and waved. He trotted over followed by one of the collies.

"Mornin' wife," he said, took the coffee and planted a kiss on her lips. He sat down by her on the step. "I've been waitin' a long time to say that. Rex became a daddy last night." Sterling scratched the dog behind the ears.

Gladys nudged the dog with a boot. Rex looked up at her smiling.

"How do you know it was him?"

"Easy to figure out, he's the one that's grinnin' and I caught him in the act awhile back."

"Does he smile like that all the time?" She asked, looking at Rex and grinning back.

"Only when he's a new father or involved in question-able activities."

"He's not the only one who's been busy in questionable activities," she responded cheekily and threw him a side-ways glance.

Sterling mimicked the dog's grin, "I had help."

He then added, "That was some night."

Gladys smiled shyly and thought back to last night. She couldn't believe how natural and totally right it felt to be with him. She'd stayed awake after he'd fallen asleep. The moon-light illuminated the room much as her mind glowed in being totally loved. He was finally hers and she didn't want to waste a minute sleeping. She traced down his body with her fingers and watched as a smile crossed his lips. He stirred against her leaving no doubt that he wanted her as much as she wanted him.

"I best get movin'. I gotta check the east pasture and make sure nothin's there before we move the herd. I already ate with Andy and I'm sure somethin's left." Sterling got up, stretched and headed towards the barn where Beauty stood saddled and waiting.

"I'll get something in town," she called and took the empty cups inside.

Gladys fired up the used Ford sedan Sterling had given her as a graduation and wedding present. She popped it into reverse and headed towards Elk City. Her Arizona family had wanted to give them privacy for their first night. But she and Sterling didn't want Bud to go to anymore expense and she was going to insist that they stay with them. Sterling told her to stock the kitchen while Estelle was in town to help her.

As she pulled into a space, she spied Bud and them going into the old Katy. She honked and Lucille came running up to her.

Lucille tackled her with a hug. "Did you have fun kissin' Sterling? When do I get to see your horse? Can I ride her? How big is the ranch?"

Gladys shut the door with her foot and hugged Lucille back.

"All in good time and yes, I want ya'll to come home with me and yes, you can ride my horse. Getting ready to eat breakfast?"

"Yep."

They walked into Mabel's Place and saw the counter was mostly empty.

Estelle and Bud were seated, blowing on their coffee and ordering breakfast. Gladys ordered pancakes and a glass of milk as did Lucille. Gladys thought the diner looked a bit rundown and not as clean as they'd kept it. The waitresses looked nice in their yellow uniforms and white aprons, but the homey feel of the place was missing.

She turned to Bud and Estelle and stated emphatically, "Sterling and I insist that you come and spend the rest of your visit with us. You've gone to all the trouble and expense to come to my graduation and our wedding. We have plenty of room and we're not taking no for an answer."

Estelle opened her mouth to object and Gladys continued.

"Bud, he wants you to look over the ranch and cattle, and Estelle I need to do some shopping. Besides," she said looking over at Lucille, "we have six new puppies."

"Puppies!" She squealed. "Can I take one home?"

Gladys shook her head no and said, "They arrived last night and can't leave their mama. Besides didn't Peggy give you one of hers?"

Lucille wiped her mouth daintily and replied, "It's my decided opinion that one cannot have too many puppies."

Bud choked on his coffee and rose to pay the bill.

"C'mon you rascal. Let's go see the puppies and leave your mama and aunty to their shopping." Lucille walked to the register and grabbed his hand. The bell above the door rang as they walked out.

Gladys finished her coffee and said, "It's so nice to see that she hasn't changed Estelle. I was scared for her when you left, but she looks so much better."

They left the café and slowly walked down the street.

"Goodness, this town has grown," Estelle exclaimed as cars and people hurried by. "Why paving the streets was only talk when we left."

"Yes, the hotel on Route 66 has put Elk City on the map," Gladys adjusted her gloves as they strolled.

"Back to Lucille," Estelle said. "She's better, but still has palpitations if she over exerts. Arizona's working out for us. Learning comes as natural to her as breathing. She told us she plans on reading every book in the Flagstaff library, including the encyclopedias. You should see the pile of books in the back seat. She read to us coming out and the trip seemed shorter."

201

Estelle paused to greet and wave to folks she knew before continuing.

"She's not strong enough to be in school and I'm sure she would correct the teacher and be a nuisance. We're going to take it slow and see how it goes with her health."

"Anyway, I'm so pleased to have this time with you," Estelle said as they walked into Miller's Goods and surveyed the shelves. "What do you need?"

"I took another quick inventory of the kitchen." Gladys rummaged in her purse and brought out a list. "A new broom and dustpan, good paring knife, and a set of canisters. We have utensils and plenty of dishes, pots and pans."

"Okay, what about groceries?" Estelle said.

"The pantry is stocked with canned goods. We need flour and sugar and dry goods; then enough food for while you're here. Most days I take my meals at the hospital and Sterling eats with Andy. When I'm not working, I'll make our meals."

"Let's pick up a ham for tonight and then visit the green grocer. We could start a small herb garden and see what vegetable starts he has that won't burn up this summer," Estelle continued as they slowed in front of the butcher. "Bud could turn the earth and build a fence for the garden and you'd be set."

"I would love to have fresh tomatoes and lettuce. Ma always kept a small garden although I didn't tend it, but I did help her plant it. It's a lovely memory I have of her."

"What an interesting quilt!" Estelle exclaimed. "I recognize some of the quilt scraps and the four patch patterns, but why the big blocks in between?" She and Gladys were at the door of the bedroom looking in.

"Remember that day when we went to the fair and quilt show?"

"I do."

"At the show there was a quilt with mismatched squares and it seemed to tell a story. It had all kinds of designs; broken dishes, log cabin, monkey wrench, to name a few. The only other quilt I have was the sampler I made with you. I decided I wanted my wedding quilt to tell my story, kinda like a map of my life. I remembered that show quilt so well because it was signed C. Simmons, Coffeyville Alabama. I always thought she might be a relative, as Pa was from Alabama."

"Anyway, back to this quilt," Gladys continued. "The big black square represents the time Ma died and the dark period when it was Pa, Jack and me. As you can see the squares got lighter, as did my heart, once I came to live with you, Bud and Lucille."

"Maybe so."

"Mama, Gladys, come see me ride a horse." Lucille stomped quickly into the house because she still wasn't allowed to run.

Her mama felt her head and watched her chest rise and fall. "Not until you've rested for a half hour and drink a big glass of water." Lucille opened her mouth to argue and then thought better or it. She grabbed Susie and sat down.

Gladys brought her a glass of cool water. "After we watch your rodeo, do you want to teach me that new game you learned from Peggy? I'm tired of Rummy."

"Sure," Lucille nodded, "I'd love to play Smut."

"That's a terrible name, but you have a deal," Gladys said.

# Chapter Thirty-five | Baby Girl

*December 1931*

Ma had always said that no wind blew as cold as a northwest wind on the prairie in winter. The sun hid behind the scudding clouds all that day. The clinic was closed after a long day. Gladys was behind schedule running the autoclave, but she knew a hot supper and Sterling waited for her when she got home. He always put her house shoes next to the fireplace so she could slip her chilled toes into the slipper's toasty warmth.

The clinic was next door to the hospital and most days it was just her and Doc. When Doc was needed elsewhere, she ran it by herself. Sometimes she assisted him at the hospital when he had surgery or rounds, but mostly she took care of inoculations and minor injuries. If she needed him, he was a phone call away.

She was locking the front door when she heard a soft knock. Switching on the porch light and pushing aside the curtains she looked through the glass and saw a huddled mountain of rags and blankets. Well, so much for a hot soup supper she thought as she opened the door.

"Come in, you'll catch your death." Moving out of the way she counted six figures as they slowly shuffled in.

The ma of the group came forward and thrust a small child towards her. "Somethin's ailin' this baby. She won't quit cryin'."

Gladys felt the screaming girl's cheek.

"This child is burning up," Gladys said. "Ya'll wait here. I'll call the doctor and be right back."

She went to her desk and removed the receiver from the phone, cranked the handle twice and waited a moment for the operator to connect. "Amy, its Gladys. I've a bit of an emergency and I need you to ring the hospital and have Dr. Sahid come here. Also, would you mind getting hold of Sterling and tell him to bring soup and all the bowls and spoons as he can muster."

The baby's cries were ear splitting. "Yes, we have a sick child, and tell Sterling we can use some blankets, too."

The wind screeched and howled intensifying the sound of the screams. The children sat with their fingers in their ears. Gladys took the child from her mother. "I'm going to examine her."

She took the child to an exam room and removed her wraps. She noted loose stool and a bright red, rashy bottom. A rectal temperature measured 102 degrees. She cleaned the baby and was drying her when Doc arrived through the back door.

He examined the child and gently stretched and rotated her foot and listened as Gladys reported her findings, then he handed her back.

"Okay," he peered through his glasses. "She's dehydrated. Wrap her up and give her baby aspirin. Then get some formula down her. You know how to make it?"

"Two parts water to one part canned milk, a tablespoon of molasses, a half teaspoon salt, and two droppers of vitamins."

"That's the ticket," he said gently and touched the baby's cheek. "I'll go talk to the family."

She took the baby who had quieted down considerably after her diaper change. "C'mon kiddo, let's make you something to eat."

She tied the baby around her in a sling to keep her warm and secure. In no time, the formula was gently warming and three bottles with nipples and rings were boiling on the other burner. She deftly lifted the bottles and nipples out of their bath with forceps to cool on a towel. She turned off the formula and added the vitamins. The baby hiccupped, woke and commenced her wails of protest.

"Hang on Baby; we just got to let it cool." She patted the baby's bottom and found Doc holding a note in an empty waiting room.

"Where did they all go?" She inquired.

"Dunno," and he handed her the note.

She unfolded it and read, "Keep her, we ain't got monee for medsin or burin."

"Keep her? They're abandoning her?" The baby started fussing. "I'll be right back." She went to the kitchen, assembled the bottles, and popped one in her mouth. The baby took it eagerly.

Walking back, she asked, "What do we do now?"

"Do about what?" Sterling blew through the front door bringing a flurry of snowflakes with his kettle of soup and basket of bowls and spoons. "It's getting colder by the minute." He looked around, "Hey, I thought I was feedin' a crowd."

"You were, they left, read this." She gestured to Doc to hand him the note. Sterling took it, read it and peered at the bundle in her arms. "Lemme feed her and you explain."

Gladys transferred the baby to Sterling and while she talked, Doc looked closely through the front window, and then took a pipe from his pocket and tobacco from another. He packed his pipe, lit it and sat down.

"So what's wrong with her?"

"I 'spect a virus. She's dehydrated and malnourished, but nothing serious." Doc replied. "The main problem is she has a club foot."

Gladys helped herself to some soup, but couldn't eat. She watched Sterling feeding the baby. They were gazing into each other's eyes. Great, she thought.

Sterling unwrapped her feet and noticed the right foot drooped and turned inward.

"Does it hurt?"

"Hmm, I think it's turning into a blizzard, and no it doesn't hurt her. I'll keep her in the hospital and when she's healthy, then she can go to the orphanage. I doubt she'll get her foot fixed," he said slyly. "Nor is she very adoptable. You say something earlier about soup?"

Sterling unplugged the child and saw she had emptied all four ounces. He deftly slung her over his shoulder and patted her back. She let out a burp and sighed to sleep.

"Where did you learn so much about babies?" Doc inquired of Sterling as he took the bowl of soup Gladys handed him.

"The orphanage and then ridin' west on the orphan train," Sterling explained. "Us older kids always had one or two younger ones to take care of."

Gladys went to the exam room to think. She knew Sterling wanted that baby. But for her, all she saw were diapers and typhoid. She didn't understand Sterling's desperation for children and had hoped she would be enough for a while. Chewing a fingernail, she remembered what he'd told her about his childhood. She knew he'd raised his sister for almost a year after their parents died, before being discovered by children's services and going to an orphanage. They were separately adopted from the orphan train. He was treated badly and overworked by the farmer who selected him. Still, she understood the hunger of wanting to be loved and having someone to love.

She heard, "We'll take her."

I knew it, Gladys thought. She hollered, "What did you say?"

"I'll take her."

"You aren't even talking it over with me? Who's going to take care of her with me working and you ranching?" She demanded.

"Quiet, you'll wake Baby Girl," Sterling admonished

"Perfect," she rolled her eyes. "You've already named her."

"If you need me, I'll be in my office," Doc interjected, puffing furiously and feigning disinterest.

"Okay, let's talk. What do you think?" The baby cooed and opened her eyes. She looked around. Sterling checked her still clean diaper and handed her to his wife. "Look at that sweet face, and I promise to do the heavy lifting."

"She's not a bale of hay."

She took the child and Baby Girl snuggled into her breast and went to sleep.

"Okay, she's sweet now that she's not hollering, but what about her foot?"

"Hell, we'll take her to the City and get it fixed."

"I don't know."

Doc had heard the exchange and with perfect timing, sauntered back in.

"Her foot isn't that bad and should be easy to correct at this point." Looking off in the distance, he said, "You two go on home. I'll check on her tonight."

"Great," Sterling excitedly clapped his hands and startled the baby awake "I'll pick my truck up in the morning and check on Baby Girl."

Gladys handed her to Doc and fetched the other two bottles. In the meantime, Doc and Sterling bundled her up. Doc tucked the bottles in his pocket and the crying child in his overcoat. "Off we go," he said and hurried out the back door. Baby Girl had started crying again but stopped in the cold air and snow.

Gladys walked briskly down the hall and heard Sterling tidying up the kitchen.

I need some air, she thought, exited the front door and started the sedan Sterling bought for her as a graduation present. I ought to drive away without him. I'm not ready for this yet.

Sterling locked the front door and stomped his way through the snow.

". . . you have every right to be upset. I know I should have talked to you, but the words were out of my mouth before I knew it." He smiled sheepishly as he got in the car and put it in gear. "I don't want any child to be without a family and in an orphanage."

She adjusted the lap quilt over both of them. "You should have talked it over with me, first. I get it that you want a family and I want that, too. But this is not what I envisioned for us right now."

Sterling drove over the train tracks that led out of town. By the siding he saw an open box car and people scrambling to get inside. Gladys was turned towards him and didn't see them.

"Then again, sometimes it's best to not over think a situation." He swallowed hard and she watched his Adam's apple bob in his throat. "I promise I'll take care of her."

"Sterling, she isn't a project and you aren't Commander Cody, out to save the world. Like I said, I don't feel settled about this and I don't want to be pushed into a decision."

"Well I can't say I ain't disappointed."

"We'll take her for now, and help her get well, but I'm not promising anything. How are you going to manage while I'm at work?"

"I'll cook and work inside until spring. Damn, I can take her with me, strapped to my back like a papoose." Sterling said excitedly, "If you'll give us a chance."

As they turned into the drive, Gladys said, "Well, this certainly puts a wrench in Christmas with the folks coming out."

"Why should it?" Sterling replied. "Lucille's been bugging us to have a baby since before we were married."

"Remember, nothing is a sure thing, Sterling."

*December 15, 1931*
*Dear Lucille,*
*How is school going? You about to graduate college yet? Ha ha! It's been cold and snowy here. How are your mama and daddy? And have you finished reading through the Flagstaff library?*
*We've been real busy. Me and Handy Andy (that's what your aunt calls him) are fixing things this winter and looking after the cattle. We have three pregnant cows and running fifteen head. Andy sleeps in the bunkhouse but eats with us.*
*Gladys is busy with the clinic.*

Can't wait until the 24th and you're here for Christmas. It'll be fun to all be together. By the way, we'll meet your train, and do we ever have a special surprise for you.

Hugs and kisses, and see you soon,

Uncle Sterling

P.S. I want a flattened dime from the train tracks as a Christmas present.

# Chapter Thirty-six | Lucille & Gracie

*Christmas 1931*

"Mama, Mama, I see 'em, I see 'em!" Lucille's nose was smashed against the train window as she waved furiously at Sterling and Gladys. "Sterling is holding somethin'. I think it's my special present. Maybe a bunny! I could bring a bunny home on the train with me.Or maybe a kitty. Daddy, is that a kitty?"

Bud and Estelle peered out and started waving, too.

"Beats me," Bud said. "Maybe a bunny; but why bring it to the station?"

Estelle took another look out the window, while the train's brakes whistled and hissed. The lumbering engines ground to a stop. "If that's a bunny or kitty, I'll eat my hat," she murmured.

Lucille ran ahead and was at the entrance to the car and urging the conductor to hurry up please and let her off. Bud and Estelle scrambled to gather the luggage and follow her.

In a flash, Lucille was off the train and hugging Sterling around his waist as he bent down to show her what was in the bundle.

Lucille turned towards the train and hollered. "Mama, come quick. It's a baby!"

Estelle dropped the luggage and ran to investigate.

"Mama, Daddy, look. Gladys and Sterling got me a baby." Lucille was holding her.

Gracie's brown curls were framed by a rabbit's skin hood. Her amber eyes looked at Lucille and then Estelle. Estelle stroked her cheek and whispered, "My, where did you come from?" Bud came up, struggling with the luggage.

He looked at his wife and daughter, dropped the luggage, embraced Gladys and slapped Sterling on the back.

"You son of a gun," he said.

"Here Daddy, you wanna hold Baby Gracie?"

Bud took the little girl from his daughter and his lips brushed her forehead. Gracie smiled and showed him a bunch of teeth before socking him on the cheek. "Prize fighter, hey?" Laughing, he handed her back to Sterling.

"I know two girls who need to get home so Santy Claus and his reindeer can come for a visit. We'll tell you all about Gracie Girl on the way." Sterling said and led the way to the car. "Ya'll get settled, while Bud and I put away the luggage."

Sterling handed Grace to Estelle, who had scooted all the way over to the other side of the car. Lucille followed and Estelle handed Gracie to Lucille, and Gladys got in last. Bud brought quilts to them from the trunk and they tucked themselves in.

Lucille sat Gracie on her lap where she faced her. Gracie and Lucille stared at each other without talking. "How did you get her?" Lucille asked once the men were in the car and they crossed the railroad tracks.

Gladys began. "This family came with a sick child and couldn't take care of her so she's staying with us for now. By her teeth we figure she's about two and a half years old. She stands but can't walk because of a bad foot so she crawls or scoots."

"Can Doc fix her foot?" Lucille asked.

"No. Sterling is going to take her to St. Anthony's in the City. From what Doc and I have read, she's going to need operations and a leg brace. He'll have to sell a heifer and a calf at least to pay for her care."

Gracie began fussing and Estelle's hands inched towards the baby.

"Lucille, why don't you hand her over to your Ma?" Estelle took the baby and Gladys handed her a bottle.

"Does she talk?" Lucille asked.

"Some, mostly she jabbers and points."

"Why did her family give her away?"

"They couldn't pay for her to get better and she was getting too big to carry around. The Ma was already expecting."

Gladys noticed Gracie's hand wrapped tight around Lucille's finger. Estelle looked at the baby with such tenderness, and she wished she felt the same way. Bud and Sterling were talking in the front seat. She put her arm around Lucille, snuggling her in close.

Gladys whispered, "You'll always be my first and best girl. I loved you from the moment I saw you."

"I loved you, too." Lucille declared back. "Can I sleep with Gracie?"

"Not yet. She's too little and sleeps in a crib."

"Gracie's a better surprise than a bunny or a puppy."

Sterling answered from the front seat, "I think so."

Gladys said nothing.

Estelle looked at her oddly and mouthed, "Are you okay?"

Gladys shook her head slightly and mouthed, "I don't think so."

# Chapter Thirty-seven | Turn Your Radio On

*Spring 1932*

"Open wide so the engine can go through the tunnel."
Sterling's mouth mirrored Gracie's as he spooned in applesauce.
"Now eat some egg and toast and I'll get us some milk. "

"Stay put," Gladys put her hand on his shoulder. "I'll get
it." She retrieved the bottle of milk from the ice box and poured
two small glasses and set them on the table.

She went into the living room and turned on the Philco
to warm up. Heading back to the kitchen she watched as Sterling undid the long dishtowel securing Gracie to her highchair
and raised up the tray.

"Well, seein' as you're more interested in playin' than
eatin' Baby Girl, let's get you cleaned up."

He took her to the sink and wiped her hands and face.
Her legs hung straight down in a brace that turned her foot
outward and connected to a straight bar that tensioned her foot
in place to straighten it.

Sterling put her down and she scooted on her bottom
over to Gladys. "Up," she held out her arms.

"No, go get your blocks and play."

Gracie frowned and scooted over to her basket of toys.
She found her baby doll and instead of cuddling her, threw her
across the room and whispered, "Bad."

The Philco hummed, crackled and came to life as The
Carter Family sang, "I got a home in Glory land." Gladys swung
her leg in time to the music as it got louder and worked on a
drunkard's path quilt block. She and Sterling had been married
for almost a year and she figured they had graduated from
newlywed status. The block was a wandering mess of pieces,
matching her mood.

She knew Sterling wanted to make Gracie theirs. But how could she commit to a child she felt so very little for? She had no maternal feelings, no desire to snuggle or read and play with the little girl. She felt nothing in her heart. I'm just a bad seed, just like Pa. She didn't know how to sort out her feelings.

She thought back to Christmas. The Arizona folks, besotted with Gracie, and Lucille couldn't get enough of her "cousin." She pulled Gracie around in the red wagon. They explored the barn, and Bud and Sterling took them for horseback rides. At night, Estelle snuggled and sang lullabies to help Gracie sleep.

All six of them went into town and had a family portrait made. Gracie loved the attention. Bud and Estelle went to Anthony's and added to her wardrobe and bought her blocks and a baby doll.

The afternoon before they left on the train that night, Bud, Sterling and Andy took the two girls on a wagon ride. The women lay down on the bed in Gladys and Sterling's bedroom. Gladys was thankful for the time to have an honest chat with Estelle.

"I can't believe how fast time has flown. It seems like we just got here and now we're leaving. That turquoise pendant goes beautifully with your eyes." Estelle continued, "Now, do you want to talk about what's bothering you?"

"I never have enough time with you and Bud, and I'm having a bit of an adjustment," Gladys explained. "I'm not head over heels in love with Gracie. Every time I change her or clean up a mess, I feel like I'm back in Leedey. I'm not ready, if ever, to have my own child."

"By the way, thank you for bringing me something pretty from Arizona," Gladys fingered her necklace. "I hope I get to visit sometime."

"You know we would love to have you visit, but I know you're all tied up with work, the ranch and now a baby. I don't know how you do it." Estelle smiled. "Besides, you got to try Mexican food."

"The same way you did at the Katy," said Gladys. "You just do it."

"I understand that. But I want you to know, I felt very little for Lucille when she was born."

Gladys turned towards her in surprise. "You, why?"

"Probably because I spent the last four months in bed because I kept bleeding," Estelle glanced down at her ample bosoms. "After she was born, you would think I would make plenty of milk for the baby, but it never came in and we both ended up crying. Finally, Bud gave her a bottle of milk. He closed the Katy for a week and took care of both of us. Sterling would talk to Bud every morning before he took off on Beauty. I saw what a good friend he was to Bud, even if they occasionally drank and smoked."

"When did you start to feel better?"

"Bud and Lucille went shopping and he came home with two window boxes full or geraniums that he hung from the front window sill of the café. He'd take Lucille out to the front porch to feed her and I could hear him talking and singing to her through the open window. I didn't want to be left out, so I went outside, too. I don't know how he found them in January."

Gladys chewed her fingernail and asked, "When did your feelings change?"

"Sterling came over one evening after hauling freight all day. In the back of the wagon, he had two rocking chairs that he deposited on the front porch. Said they were a present from him to us." Estelle dropped her voice, "The only memory he has of his mother is being rocked to sleep with Baby Beth Anne in a big rocker."

Gladys sat up. "Sterling has never shared any of that with me. Now I know why he insisted we bring those rockers to the ranch. So you think I will learn to love Gracie?"

"I do," said Estelle. "She's a lovely child and you can always come to Arizona for a visit."

"Sterling seems to be happiest taking care of someone," Gladys observed, getting out of bed. "I hear the girls laughing downstairs."

"I'll finish packing and then help you get supper on the table," Estelle got up, smoothed the quilt and fluffed the pillows.

"I'm putting out leftovers for a cold supper. I'll make you some sandwiches and put coffee in the thermos," Gladys hugged Estelle. "Life is always better with you around."

"You better get downstairs before those men and two little girls take over the kitchen." Estelle returned her hug and watched Gladys leave. Her brow furrowed with worry as she remembered Gladys at thirteen, when she first came to them, neglected, overworked and unloved. Years of care and attention had transformed her into a lovely woman.

But now, she detected an edge, and she prayed the Simmons family history would not repeat itself between Gladys and Gracie.

# Chapter Thirty-eight | Black Duster

*Spring 1932*

Why was Beauty so skittish leaving the ranch? Sterling gently touched him with a whip letting him know who was in charge. The sky was clear with no sign of a windstorm. Early spring flowers danced gently in a soft warm breeze. It promised to be a fine day to scout the fence line and fix any breaks.

Andy was hoeing the kitchen garden for Gladys. She was anxious to plant her summer vegetable starts once the soil was loosed and manure worked in well. Gladys had been up since before dawn washing and hanging out the laundry. He had fixed Gracie's corn flakes and a small glass of milk before he left.

The weather dominated conversation when he went into town. A freak two-day dust storm at the end of February had caused the old timers to scratch their head and comment it was like nothing like they'd ever seen. A few head of cattle belonging to Mr. Macon had been caught in it and died. Upon opening them up, their lungs were full of dust. March brought two more black blizzards.

Maybe the clear sky this April morning heralded a fresh start. Still, he was glad Bud's family was in Arizona. With Lucille's compromised health, they didn't need to contend with the dusty elements here.

As he and Beauty clopped along, he stopped to straighten a fence pole and tighten the barbed wire. Tumbleweeds or Russian thistles were the enemy of a good fence, and with his hoe he hacked at a group of tumbleweeds that had caused it to lean. When he and Andy had put up the barbed wire two years ago, the work seemed easy. Both of them had been proud of the strong fence around the ranch pastures.

Moving along he thought back to Gladys and their argument yesterday. Gracie had been asleep and Andy was mending tack in the barn so they had a rare moment of privacy.

He'd started by saying, "With Gracie doin' so well, don't you think it's' time to give her a brother or sister? We've got some extry set aside now and ..."

"So are you going to birth and nurse these children? Or are we just going to pluck another one from thin air, like last time?" She interrupted. "The only reason we have some extra is because of me. Last time I checked, the ranch still needed the money I make."

"I thought it was our money. Good Lord, Gladys, ever since Gracie came, you've never let me forget that it was my idea and you just went along with the notion." Sterling stood up and poured himself more coffee. "It's been a while and you have yet to accept her. FACE IT, SHE'S OURS!"

Sterling took his cup and slammed the door as he left. He never considered harming a woman and he was not about to start today, but he just did not understand her reluctance or coldness towards Gracie. Sure, Gladys met her needs, but she did not bestow extra kisses or hugs just because she was her mother. As a child, she was neglected, and he didn't understand how she could be so reserved towards their daughter.

He'd always wanted a houseful of kids and felt that his desires ought to matter for something. He'd loved Gladys since she was fifteen and had waited for her until she and her family were ready for him to marry her. True, he wished she were less interested in her calling and more interested in being on the ranch with him and Gracie, but the money she made had helped him build up the herd and pay Andy decent wages.

She had never denied him and seemed to enjoy their lovemaking as much as he did, or at least that's what she said. But still, ever since Gracie came into their lives, she held herself so close. He missed her spontaneity and brightness that lit up his world when they were courting and first married.

He was sorry he had brought up the subject of money, but they could make it just fine if she worked less. He knew how much her education meant and he would never suggest that she quit working.    It fulfilled a deep hollow place inside, but why couldn't she make more room for him and Gracie.

He noticed another weak link in the fence. He checked the posts, and they were firm in the ground, but the wire was loose. Untying the fence puller, he ratcheted the section and pulled the wires tight before continuing on with Beauty and commencing his musing.

He couldn't be prouder of Gracie. She wore a barred brace all the time and it amazed him how she moved around. She sideways walked swinging one foot in front the other. She used the gadget he and Andy had made to help her balance and walk. Sometimes she scooted on her bottom to get around quicker. She was greased lighting whether she scooted or walked. He tightened the brace at night using a hex key. Gradually, the tension was increased stretching her muscles. It was his hope that someday soon she would run and skip like any other little girl.

His greatest joy was when she accompanied him on chores around the ranch, pulled in a red wagon. She had her own rake and shovel and loved to help him or Andy muck out the barn and spread fresh straw in the stalls. He'd given her a little calf she called Cow that she curried with a small brush and comb. She helped him feed the stock, but when it came time to feed the chickens or gather eggs she'd scurry as best she could into the house. An old biddy pecked her once and she hadn't forgotten.

He looked back at the house and saw Gracie in her overalls, helping Andy hoe the garden. She was jabbering away and pointing. Andy haunched down and picked up something from the dirt. Sterling figured it must be a worm. They'd have to dig and fill a coffee can with dirt and worms the next time it rained and take her fishing. He chuckled at the thought of her delight.

He hopped off Beauty again. Tumbleweeds packed a section and he knew it would take the better part of an hour to clear them. Again, he looked towards the house. The laundry flapped on the line and Gladys had Gracie in her little red flexible flyer and was pulling her around the yard. He felt that this was a small encouraging step. Maybe the smart thing to do was wait until she accepted their daughter more fully, before talking about having more kids.

He took a long drink of water from his burlap encased canteen and started breaking up the weeds. After chopping them into smaller pieces, they easily blew through the fence and scattered their seeds to the wind. He tightened the loose wire.

As he got back on Beauty, the horse turned and looked at him reproachfully. Sterling gave him his head just to see where he would go. No surprise to him that Beauty wanted to go home. The wind was picking up, but there was not a cloud or haze in the sky.

"C'mon boy, let's finish the last two sections and then I'll give you some extry oats and a long drink of water when we get home."

He touched him lightly with his spurs and turned his head back towards the fence. Beauty tried once again to head towards the barn.

"You know somethin' I don't? Let's fix that section I see saggin' down yonder and if you still want to go in, we'll talk."

Sterling did notice the wind picking up. He took another long drink from his canteen and poured the rest of the water in his felt hat so Beauty could have a drink. He replaced his hat and pulled his handkerchief over his mouth and hacked away at the weeds. Beauty stayed close by, nibbling at the grass. The growth was substantial and old tumbleweeds were mixed in with new growth. Sterling chopped, sweated, and swore for a good hour.

He only looked up when Beauty clamped his teeth on his shoulder. He'd been nickering for a good amount of time, but he was driven to get this patch cleared and ignored him.

"All right you durn horse, what is it now."

Sterling looked around to the North. The blue sky was quickly being snuffed out by a boiling wall of black dust. It seemed to touch the sky, all the way down to the earth and moved faster than a blizzard. He looked back at the house and saw Gladys frantically bringing in laundry and waving at him. Gracie sat in the wagon and waved a kerchief. Andy rode back and forth from the near pasture to the barn gathering the herd.

Sterling dropped his tools, jumped on Beauty's back and lit out for the barn and house. The wind hit and the grit came at them from every direction. Beauty screamed and he jumped off and tried to lead Beauty in the direction of home. He jerked and pulled, but Sterling held fast to the reins with his glove covered hands. He felt if he got separated from the horse, all would be lost. But, Beauty stumbled blindly. He pulled first to the left and then to the right. It seemed all his instincts and horse sense was gone with the blow. Sterling jerked the bridle and yelled at him to move. If they were to make it back, he had to rely on his own human sense.

Sterling had no idea how long he'd been pulling Beauty through the storm. It seemed the day must be heading towards night because it was darker. His throat was raw and he could hardly breathe. He kept clearing dirt from Beauty's nose, but his heaving sides and sweaty flanks told Sterling he was having a terrible time breathing. Suddenly, Beauty shuddered and pitched to his side. Sterling lay down beside him and put his arm over him. He placed his handkerchief over Beauty's nose and mouth and tried to forget his own pain so he could comfort his horse. Perhaps by hunkering down, one of them could outlast the storm.

Gladys and Andy stayed up all night in silence drinking coffee. They wanted to go out and search, but knew it was as futile as going out in a snow blizzard to try and find someone. Nevertheless, every window was lit with candles or a gas lamp to guide him home. Gladys rocked Gracie and cried as her lips moved in a soundless petition to her Ma and Jesus. If only Sterling made it back, she would give him dozens of children and be nicer.

Gracie's head was wet with her tears in the morning.

Andy rode to the fence line where they last saw Sterling. Tumbleweeds and dirt obscured any evidence of repair. He rode further down the line and noticed a mound in the middle of the furthermost pasture. Riding to it and digging with his hands, he uncovered Sterling's head and torso with his arm still around Beauty.

Andy tied him to the back of his horse and made his way to the house.

He looked up and saw Gladys, pulling Gracie in her wagon, trudging through the red silt to meet them.

*April 21, 1932*
*Dear Diary,*

*Daddy left on the train for Oklahoma because Sterling and Beauty are dead as doornails. Damn, damn and double damn. I'm so mad I could spit and cry and spit again. Really dead. The dust got to them when they were out at the fence line. I don't know what to do ⋯ I'm staying here with Ma as she can barely get outta bed because her gall bladder is messing up. Me and Peggy are gonna take care of her while daddy is gone.*

*I've known Sterling my whole life. He was my best friend in Oklahoma and taught me how to play rummy and poker. Mama never did find out about the poker. He always ate with us and he was supposed to be my forever Uncle, and now he's dead. I look at the ring and can't believe he's gone.*

*I've never been this sad, not even when I was sick. I feel empty inside and the world is all wrong. I hope the dust doesn't swallow Daddy, Gladys and Gracie. I would be half an orphan. Damn, hell, and poop.*

*(Gladys' Diary Entry)*

*I killed Sterling. Heaven knows Gracie complicated our lives. I wanted more time with just him and me before any children showed up. He rode out upset and I didn't call him back to kiss him or tell him I loved him.*

*We waited so long to love each other fully. And now he's gone, and I don't know what to do with his baby or this ranch.*

# Chapter Thirty-nine | Bud & Gracie

*Spring 1932*

"Unky Ba," Gracie cried when Bud walked through the door. Scooting towards him and waving her hands she said, "Up, Up!"

"Hey, Monkey," Bud picked her up and noticed her clothes and hair were crusty with food and there was a God awful smell in the room. Gladys rocked silently and took no notice of him or Gracie.

He looked towards the kitchen and noticed dishes and food piled in the sink and the flies slowly circling.

"Shoo, shoo," Gracie said and waved her hands to swish them away.

Under his breath he muttered, "Geez Louise, this is worse than I thought; reminds me of the home place when Ma and them died."

"Huh?" Gracie said.

"Nothin' Sweetheart."

Ignoring the kitchen, his eyes traveled to the living room where Sterling's wooden box lay on sawhorses. By the stench he knew Sterling's body had not been embalmed.

"See, Daddy." Gracie said.

Bud walked over and and saw Sterling's jaw was tied shut with a rag and quarters were placed on his eyes to keep them closed. Cotton wads were stuffed in his nose and ears. He had on a clean pair of jeans and shirt, but the ever-present flies circled his head.

"Shoo, shoo."

They looked in and Gracie pointed, "Daddy stinky."

Hugging her he said, "I know, Baby Girl."

Bud looked over at Gladys, but she still rocked like she was in a trance.

Gracie struggled to get down and she sideways stomped over to where the lid of the coffin lay against the sawhorses. She looked up at Bud, "Help."

"You're right. Daddy's gone and we need to get him buttoned up tight." Bud put the lid on the coffin.

He heard Andy yell from outside, "Batten down the hatches!"

With a crash the sky went dark and the wind shrieked like it was alive with voices. The ranch dogs howled, meeting the pitch of the winds. Gladys stood wild-eyed and her voice rose to meet the howling of the dogs; her hair standing on end, alive with static electricity. A ball of fire rolled down the chimney before breaking into three smaller balls and rolled around the room before touching briefly and disappearing up the chimney.

Bud and Gracie's hair rose up, too. Gracie stood still and sucked her thumb. He tried to pick her up, but they both received a shock and her brace glowed blue. He grabbed her and yanked the brace off by her shoes and threw it across the room, being careful to not touch the metal.

Gracie began to cry so he gently placed her on the divan, before picking up Gladys and doing the same. He sat in between them and patted them both. Gradually Gladys's howls turned to hiccups and Gracie stopped crying.

"Unky Ba?"

"Sweetheart, I know you want to know what in hell happened and I'm rackin' my Unky Ba brain tryin' to come up with a reason. I think those balls of fire were lightnin', but I've never seen it before. It caused the metal of your brace to turn blue and shocked us."

"Oh." Gracie yawned and scooted even closer. She pulled up the little blanket that Estelle gave her for Christmas and went to sleep. Gradually Gladys became heavy in his arms. He moved Gracie down and laid Gladys on the opposite end of the divan and covered her with an old quilt.

"I think I'll put this room to rights," Bud whispered. He couldn't sleep and he felt a dark chasm beckoning. The enormity of the tragedy threatened to overtake him, and he knew he couldn't give into the darkness.

He lit the burners on the stove and filled up big pans of water for washing and cleaning from the pump at the sink. He worked through the night and thought of the good times he and Sterling had as ranch hands. It was honest hard work and there was nothing as satisfying as riding and singing to the cattle out on the prairie under a big night sky.

He noticed a circular rope and nails that were hammered in strategic places around the room. "That must be for the laundry."

Even though he kept getting shocked, he strung the rope crosswise and hung-up the clean clothes. With the laundry done and dishes washed he put on a pot of beans, stirred up some cornmeal pancakes and lay strips of bacon on the hot griddle. He shut his mind of Sterling and concentrated on taking care of the girls.

The aroma woke Gracie and she got down and scooted to him, "Hungwy, Unky Ba."

"I bet you are. Let's get you in your chair because in a minute breakfast will be done."

He took her to the sink and gave her face and hands a lick and a promise and plopped her in the highchair. He blew on a piece of bacon and gave it to her. Gracie lost no time chewing it.

Gladys had woken up and resumed silently rocking in her chair. During the night the wind had died down. Bud took her a plate of breakfast food and placed it on the table next to her. He turned on the radio and eventually, Bob Wills and the Texas Playboys fiddled through the speaker.

He took his plate and coffee and sat down by Gracie. She'd been stuffing pancake and bacon into her mouth and chewing as fast as she could. She looked at him but kept on eating.

"Hey, slow down, Pardner. Let's chase that down with somethin' to drink"

He poured her a glass of milk. He held it for her as she gulped it down and said, "More."

"Yes ma'am. You obviously are a woman that knows her own mind."

She drank another glassful, burped and patted her round tummy.

"Okay Pardner, how about a bath. I'll wash you before the dishes."

He put a big kettle on the stove to heat. He slipped her shirt off and then he took down her panties and noticed her bottom was red with hand imprints.

"What on earth happened to your bottom?"

Gracie pointed at herself and then Gladys, "Bad, Mama 'pank me."

"What? "

"Mama 'pank me.

Bud gulped down his anger and prepared her bath. Last thing this baby needed was to sit in water that was too hot. He tested it and sat her gently in the sink. He soaped her hair and with care washed her face and the rest of her. Gracie kicked and chased the soap and washcloth with her hands. Bud rinsed and wrapped her in a towel. They went upstairs and he dressed her in a pair of short overalls.

"I ain't putting that brace on you today. Let's go find Andy."

Gracie smiled, "Andy, yay."

Bud tried to carry her and Andy's breakfast, but he couldn't get the door open. He put both down and pushed. He was able to get his head out and look around. He saw that red dirt was piled against the house, doors and barn. A fine silt covered the yard of the ranch.

"What a mess," he said and opened the door with a shove.

Gracie scooted over and stuck her own head out. "Meth," she said.

Balancing Gracie and the hot cakes and coffee they went to the outbuildings and both hollered for Andy. He came jogging out of the barn.

Any spied the food and gratefully took it

"That coffee sure hits the spot." Andy chucked Gracie under the chin.

"Thank you for what you've done for Sterling," Bud said.

"Fanks," Gracie struggled to be put down and pointed to her wagon.

"Mind doin' the breakfast dishes?" Andy asked handing his empty plate to Bud.

"Not a bit."

Andy picked up Grace and put her in the wagon and started pulling her around the drifts and tumbleweeds.

Bud balanced the dishes on the watering trough and joined the walk.

Hay was spread in the bottom and Andy stopped and pulled out two straws and offered one to Bud.

"Sorry, but I'm out of chewing tobacco."

"Andy!" Gracie commanded and scooted forward trying to make the wagon move.

Andy took the handle and the two men walked around the yard.

"After we found him, we took him to the house and together cleaned him up. I made him a coffin because she wouldn't let me call the undertaker. Then I called you folks."

Bud scratched the dirt with his toe boot and chewed his straw.

"We put the lid on last night. I'm gonna take him into town today and get him buried proper. Can I leave Pardner with you? It'll take me awhile to sort things out with Gladys."

"Sure, we've got plenty to keep us busy. We'll start with a ride in the wagon and see where the day takes us." Andy put his cowboy hat on Gracie.

Gracie shook her head and peered at them.

Andy continued. "After we tended to him, I hadn't seen either Gladys or Gracie, until you came out this morning."

Bud patted him on the shoulder, "You need anything in town?"

"Just tobacco," Andy scratched his chin. "Other than that, I'm okay. Me and Gracie have a few stalls to muck out. Where's your shovel, Gracie?"

"Daddy's shobel."

"Of course." Andy pulled her to the barn.

Bud turned towards the house and Gladys.

# Chapter Forty | Gladys & Bud

1932

Her breakfast plate was empty. She felt so hollow inside. Looking out the window she saw how natural Bud was with Gracie. Her eyes felt so bleary and gritty. She turned and looked as Bud walked in and she broke her silence.

"I've thought about it, Bud. I ain't gonna lose my mind over this, but I don't want anything more to do with this ranch. I want to bury Sterling in a cemetery not on the land, so I guess we'll have to take him to the undertaker."

"Sounds reasonable," Bud said.

"I need to get death certificates at the courthouse and I'm gonna give Gracie to the orphan's home. She was Sterling's child, not mine and I ain't fit to be a mother anyways."

"Whoa Gladys, all these decisions don't have to be made at once." Bud sat down opposite her and handed her a fresh cup of coffee.

"No, I think they do. I hope Andy wants this god forasaken place 'cause I don't." Gladys gulped her coffee down. "I'll take a room in town and work with Doctor Sahib."

Bud got up and took their cups to the sink. He slowly and deliberately finished the breakfast dishes. He leaned against the wall.

"I got a better idea; you take Gracie." Gladys stood and stretched and sat back down. "Lucille has always wanted a sister. I'll sign the ranch over to Andy, Gracie over to you, and move into town and work."

Bud sat down opposite of her and rubbed his hands on his jeans. "Sounds like a lonely life to me. Perhaps you've been strong for so long and your happiness with Sterling was so short lived. Let's take care of him and then we'll talk."

"I know you're gonna want me to move to Arizona, but I've made up my mind and I ain't leavin' him." Gladys said slipping into her childhood speech.

235

"Bit," Bud said using his pet name for her. "He's gone and he wouldn't want you to stay, just to put flowers on his grave and be miserable. Let's get him in the ground."

Gladys walked over to the coffin with her head down. Quietly she patted the lid of the coffin. "I'm sorry Sterling, for everythin'." She looked up at Bud. "Okay."

"I'll go get Andy." Bud went outside and noticed the air was still.

The two men came into the house and Gracie clomped in holding a kitty.

The kitty jumped and Gracie hitched after it yelling, "Kitty, pwetty kitty."

The men lifted the coffin and walking backward Bud pushed open the door as he struggled with the head of the casket. Gracie ran under it chasing the kitty.

Gladys caught and shook her. "Be still, you'll upset Daddy." Gladys pulled down the straps of her overalls.

"No, Mama." Gracie struggled to get away.

Gladys put her across her lap. Her jaw jutted out and her eyes narrowed. It seemed she was almost in a trance.

"No. Mama, be good," Gracie wailed.

Bud motioned for Andy to put the casket down.

"Gladys," He stopped her hand and Gracie ran to Andy who scooped her up and took her outside where he straightened her overalls. Gracie escaped and went back in the house.

"Here kitty, pwetty kitty." The kitten came onto the living room, Gracie caught her and defiantly plopped down on the lid of her daddy's coffin.

Gladys once again hung her head and whispered, "I'm turnin' into Pa."

"But you don't have to be mean like him."

"I'm awfully afraid it's too late." She rummaged in a drawer by the divan and looked into a mirror she held in her hand. "I look into this mirror and I see his sneering face. I'm him and I want to kick and scream and act ugly."

She looked at her brother. "I'm so angry, I can't be nice. I finally understand what was broken inside him; too much loss, so much grief."

Gladys finger combed her hair and braided it. "I can't take one more thing. My heart is too sore, and I feel like I'm gonna explode."

"It's never too late." He took her hands and held them palms up, looking into her blue eyes. "I choose everyday not to be like him. Something happened that made him twisted and stained inside. Come home with me and be with Estelle. Let us love you and give you time to heal."

"I can't cry."

"You will."

Gladys sighed, resigned. "Let's go into town. We can care of Sterling and go to the courthouse.

"That's the spirit," Bud said. "Does this mean you and Gracie are comin' to Arizona?"

"Only if you agree to raise her, and then I guess it's time to leave Oklahoma." Gladys continued, "I need to see Dr. Sahib."

She stood up and started looking for her hat and purse. She found them by the front door and said, "Thanks Bud."

A muscle moved in Bud's jaw. "A family takes care of one another. We'll all get through this."

Bud whistled for Andy. The truck was by the front door. Gladys, Andy, Gracie and Bud lifted Sterling and gently placed the coffin in the truck. Andy and Gracie waved as Bud and Gladys slowly drove away.

"Bye Daddy," Gracie whispered.

Gladys sold the ranch to Andy for one dollar. He insisted on buying the cattle and Sterling's truck. He would send her ten dollars every month that he could, until his debt was paid. Gladys wanted to outright give him everything and be done with the whole outfit, but Andy said no. He had his pride and insisted on a fair price for the cattle and truck.

She would miss two things on the ranch: the front porch swing and the stock tank where ahe and Sterling took swims in the dark and starry night.

A week later Gladys, Bud and Gracie loaded up Gladys' car. Gracie and Kitty sat in back eating Rice Krispy treats and sharing sips of water from a canning jar. Gladys and Bud had a strong box between them. Andy waved and Gracie waved back. As they drove Gladys kept an eye on the weather, hoping the sky would stay clear.

Bud smiled, "I think I've made this drive before."

And he turned onto the road west that led home to Estelle and Lucille.

*The End*

# Favorite Recipes from Gladys' Recipe Box

# Crazy Chocolate Cake with Powdered Sugar Frosting.

*(This was made once or twice a week.)*

Sift together:

      3 cups flour

      2 cups sugar

      1/3 cup cocoa

      2 teaspoons soda

      1 teaspoon salt

Make 2 wells and add:

      First well:

          ¼ cup vinegar and 1 ½ teaspoons vanilla

      Second well:

          1 1/3 cup oil

Pour 4 cups coffee or water over the mixture and mix well, about 200 strokes.

Pour into 2 prepared 13 by 9 inch pans and cook in a moderate (350 degrees) oven for 25-30 minutes.

Frost when cool.

# Buttercream Frosting

      3 ¾ cup powdered sugar
      ½ stick of soft butter
      3 to 4 Tablespoons of canned milk
      1 teaspoon vanilla extract

Add 3 Tablespoons cocoa powder or more for chocolate frosting and a little extra canned milk.

Combine all ingredients and beat for 2-3 minutes until smooth.

Beat at medium speed until creamy.

Frosts a cool cake. If you have extra frosting, save up to a week in the icebox.

# Apricot or Peach Cobbler

(works for most fruit)
(Gladys tripled the recipe.)

4 cups canned fruit drained, save juice.

Place fruit in 11 by 7 inch pan.

Combine together in a bowl, mixture will be lumpy:

      ½ cup brown sugar

      1 scant teaspoon of salt

      ½ teaspoon of lemon juice or vanilla

      ½ cup oatmeal

      ½ cup flour

      1/3 cup soft butter

      2/3 teaspoon of cinnamon

Crumble topping over fruit.

Bake in a 350 degree oven.

Check at 30 minutes, topping should be crispy, but not burnt.

Serve with cold cream poured over the top.

6-8 servings

*(Save juice as it can be used as simple syrup for malts and shake.)*

# Fried Green Tomatoes

Slice 3 green tomatoes thinly and dredge in a mixture of salt, pepper and flour.

Cook in a moderately hot skillet with bacon fat. Add more fat if needed.

*These cook quickly so watch and don't let them burn. You want them as crisp as possible. Be sure to turn them so both sides have a chance to crisp. Should only take a minute or two on each side.*

Serve hot with bacon, biscuits, gravy, and eggs.

# Mattie's Biscuits

> 2 cups flour
> 1 teaspoon of salt
> 1 teaspoon sugar
> 1 teaspoon baking powder
> ½ teaspoon soda

Mix together and cut in ¼ cup shortening or lard, but do not overmix dough.

Add ¾ cup buttermilk to make soft dough. Knead about 6 times.

Roll out dough to a ½ inch thick. Using a small empty tin can, cut biscuits into circles. Melt 1 Tablespoon butter in a 9-inch square pan. Lightly dredge biscuits in melted butter and crowd them in the pan.

Cook 450 degrees for 12-14 minutes.

# How to make buttermilk:

1 cup milk

Add 1 Tablespoon lemon juice or vinegar to sour the milk.

Wait 5 minutes before using as buttermilk.

Real buttermilk works best.

# Gladys' Cornbread

Grease 9-inch pan with bacon grease. Heat oven to 400 degrees. *(400 degrees is a hot oven)*

Beat together in large bowl:

> ¼ cup lard or grease
>
> 1 cup milk
>
> 1 large egg

Sift together and then add to wet ingredients:

> 1 ¼ cups cornmeal
>
> 1 cup flour
>
> 1 Tablespoon baking powder
>
> ½ teaspoon salt

Stir until dry ingredients are moistened and pour batter into prepared pan. Mixture will be lumpy.

Cook 20-25 minutes.

# Fried Chicken

Catch, kill, pluck and singe bird or use a prepared bird. Save gizzard, liver, and heart to fry.
Cut bird into 8 or 9 pieces.

Wash and pat dry.

Sift together:

> 1 ½ cups flour
>
> 1 Tablespoon paprika
>
> 2 Tablespoons salt
>
> 1 Tablespoon pepper
>
> 2 teaspoons celery powder
>
> ½ teaspoon thyme

Dredge chicken and extra bits in the flour mixture.

Heat ½ inch of lard in a good size skillet on medium high. Brown on all sides and then cover skillet and cook on medium low. Simmer for about 20 minutes.

*Uncover and turn chicken to brown the skin. Resist the urge to keep turning. Chicken crisps up at the end.*

## Cream Gravy

*Use same pan as chicken to make cream gravy.*

Add scant handful of flour to 3-4 Tablespoon of fat and to the crunches in the skillet.

*When paste is made, add canned or fresh milk until desired consistency. If gravy is too thick, add water or broth until you have desired consistency.*

Add salt and pepper to taste.

Serve with chicken and biscuits and green beans with onions and mashed potatoes.

# Estelle's Pancakes

Make buttermilk, (*2 cups canned milk, minus 2 Tablespoons. Add 2 Tablespoons vinegar or lemon juice and wait five minutes.*) or use fresh milk and set aside.

Combine:
> 2 ¼ cups flour
> 2 Tablespoons sugar
> 2 teaspoons baking powder
> 1 teaspoon soda
> ¾ teaspoon salt
> 2 eggs
> 4 Tablespoons softened butter or lard

Whisk egg and fat into the buttermilk. Pour flour mixture into the wet and whisk until lumps are gone. Add flour, a tablespoon at a time, if mixture is too thin. Add extra milk, a tablespoon at a time, if mixture is too thick.

Heat a large griddle over medium heat, grease. Pour 1/8 to 1/4 cups of batter onto griddle. Turn when bubbles appear. Flip and cook the underside until golden brown.

Serve with syrup or molasses.

# Revival Rice Casserole to feed a Crowd

In a large pan with lid, fry together:
>1 lb. of ground beef
>
>2 Tablespoons fat
>
>1 minced small onion
>
>2 cups diced celery

Add:
>1 can of corn or green beans
>
>¼ cup soy sauce or less
>
>1 cup rice
>
>1 cup of stock
>
>1 recipe of white sauce

Add white sauce to casserole with beef or chicken stock. Stir well and cover.

Cook at 325 for 1 ½ to 2 hours. Feeds 12-15. Add more stock, if needed.

# White sauce

2-3 Tablespoons flour
¼ teaspoon salt
¼ teaspoon pepper
¼ (scant) butter
1 cup milk

Melt butter over low heat. Stir in dry ingredients. Stir milk in slowly until it comes to a boil, stir constantly for one minute.

# Peanut Butter Cookies

Gladys baked these for the threshers. Peanut butter was relatively new and a real treat for Gladys and Jack. Makes 30-36 cookies.

Heat oven to 375 degrees, a moderately hot oven.

Mix together:
> ¾ cup peanut butter
> ½ cup lard or butter
> 1 ½ cups brown sugar
> 2 Tablespoons milk
> 1 Tablespoon vanilla
> 1 egg

Sift together:
> 1 ¾ cups of flour
> ¾ teaspoon baking soda
> 1 teaspoon salt
> Grease baking sheet.

Beat peanut butter, lard, brown sugar, milk, and vanilla in large bowl until blended.

Beat in egg.

Sift together flour, baking soda and salt. Gradually add dry ingredients to creamed mixture and mix until just blended.

Cool for an hour in icebox or refrigerater.

Dough by a rounded tablespoonful, 2 inches apart onto baking sheet. Flatten slightly in a crisscross pattern using tines of fork.

*If dough sticks to fork, place it in icy water between smashes.*

Sprinkle tops with a bit of plain sugar.

Cook 8- 10 minutes. Cool and try not to eat them all at once.

*Gladys doubled the recipe. Consider serving with peanut butter and jelly sandwiches, yummy.*

# FAMILY PHOTOS

Family homestead outside of Leedey, Oklahoma.
Early 1900's

Schoolhouse in the country outside of Leedey.
My grandmother, Estel Lee Wilson Simmons is 5 years old.
The photo was shot in 1916 or 17.

Picture of the Simmons Family,
one of the family photos behind the story of Gladys.
1918 or 19.

Photograph that was the inspiration for Sterling and Bud
participating in cowboy round-up.

Lee B. Wilson, my great-grandfather. He did survive the loss of four children, two from typhoid. His wife, Mattie, died from typhoid at the same time. (1922) He did whip my grandmother with a belt when she served cornbread instead of biscuits for supper.

Baptism in the creek outside of Leedey.
Early 1900's.

Katy Coffee Shop in Elk City. Early 1930's.

Betty Lucille Simmons on her father's team of horses.
He would later trade his team for a 1934 Dodge
to drive his family to Arizona.

Ready for church. My grandparents, Cliff and Estel.
My mother, Betty, is 8 or 9 at the time.

Simmons-Neel family on a trip to Oklahoma from California. Cliff has his hand on his sister Elsie's shoulder. My grandmother is holding my baby sister. My mother is beside her. I am the little girl beside my older brother and sister. My brother, David, hasn't been born yet. My dad, as usual, is taking the picture.

## Acknowledgements

It's hard to believe it's been ten years since I enrolled in Dr. Vorndran's Creative Writing Class at Pima Community College. I had no idea that my submissions that semester would culminate in a book.

After twenty three years of teaching in a private school, I, myself, needed an education in the public school world. I couldn't have been more delighted with what I was reading. A Prayer for Owen Meaney, Dogsbody and other examples of good writing challenged my thinking. We discussed our readings and participated in writing exercises. These young people took an interest in me and what I had to say, and likewise, I loved reading their stories and taking them to lunch.

I never met a kinder or sweeter group of people as when I was no longer a teacher; I was a fellow student with a lot to learn from my peers and instructors.

I kept writing, and when Dr. Vorndran moved on to teach Honors, he assured us his replacement was an exceptional teacher. Dr. Steven Salmoni became my friend and chief encourager. He always brought more out of my writing than I knew was there. He met with me during office hours and worked with me to complete the arc of my story.

I cannot say enough good things about Genevieve Max and Kathryn Bennett. They are dear friends whom I met at Pima. We formed a writing group and have been meeting for six years. They have teased details and dialogue from my writing and have been honest in pointing out what need to change. Esther Bennett, Kathryn's mom opened up her home every week, at least, and read our stories.

Another thanks to encouragers along the way: Renee, Jamison, Krista, Cheryl, August, Marcella, Jeri, Julie, Nancy, and Trixi. A special thank you to Mary Moore and Donna Douglas who both read earlier versions of the story, and frequently inquired about how I was doing, invited me to swim, meet for coffee.

Anna Weiss, my daughter, read <u>Gladys</u> frequently and offered suggestions. My husband, Tom, proofed, caught mistakes, and challenged my use of words that were out of step with what I wanted to convey. My son, David, designed the book and cover, and put the book together when I had no idea what I was doing.

My mom, Betty Neel, on whom I modeled the character of Lucille, offered astounding historical data. She lived through the depression in Altus Oklahoma and provided me with answers to questions only a living witness could provide. She thought every word I wrote was genius. I love you Mama.

Thank you to my niece, Megan Rose, who told me she wanted to know how white people lived during that time. My two sisters, Rebecca Lee, who died in 2016, and Mary Beth who are nothing like Daisy and Ivy. My life is better because we have been on this long life journey together until death do us part. Becky, you were my first friend, and Mary Beth, you are my best friend.

Thank you for reading this book.

Display type is set in Aphrosine

Text type is set in Iowan Old Style

Book & cover designed by David Weiss

CPSIA information can be obtained
at www.ICGtesting.com
Printed in the USA
LVHW111513270921
698832LV00005B/100